Also in this series

DAVID ROSS AND BOB CATTELL

CARLTON

THIS IS A CARLTON BOOK

Text and illustrations copyright © Carlton Books Limited 2010

This edition published in 2010 by Carlton Books Limited
A division of the Carlton Publishing Group
20 Mortimer Street, London W1T 3JW

First published in 1999 by André Deutsch

A catalogue record for this book is available from the British
Library.

1 3 5 7 9 10 8 6 4 2

ISBN: 978-1-84732-549-5

Printed in the UK by CPI Mackays, Chatham, ME5 8TD

Bob Cattell was born in the Fens and now lives in Suffolk.
He combines his job as a copywriter with writing children's
books about football and cricket – including the Glory
Gardens series. He is a lifelong Aston Villa supporter.

David Ross was somehow always the reserve in his school
football team, which gave him lots of time to observe the
game. He loves to hate supporting Heart of Midlothian
and has written numerous other books for children.

1
DRIVING PASSION

The feeling was unbelievable. Speed: 140 mph and still rising; acceleration: out of this world. The stubby little gear stick nestled in his hand as the long straight streamed past and the bend came into sight. He eased off the power, let the car edge over to the outside of the track, then shifted down a gear, pulled into the bend and settled back for another blistering surge as the next straight swung into view.

The car was a dream. Thomas Headley was literally laughing with pleasure as he streaked along only a few inches above the tarmac. The racer's steering wheel felt tiny in his hands after his Saab; its response to the slightest movement made him concentrate hard, harder even than on the football pitch. Through his helmet he could hear and feel the roar of the big three-litre Cosworth engine that was thrusting his vehicle forward at a mile every 25 seconds. In the mirror he saw another car behind him, moving out of the bend; then it was gone as he smoothed his way left, right through a tight chicane. The track was his, and he was the king of it.

'I want more. Lots more,' he said as he was helped out of the car by the pit attendants. With a final rasp of the engine, Jason Le Braz pulled up behind him.

'Good, eh?' said Jason, grinning up at Thomas.

F3000 racing was Jason's new passion. He'd persuaded Thomas to come along to the Silverwood circuit to try it out – although, in all honesty, Thomas didn't take a lot of persuading. They'd arrived in a helicopter belonging to one of Jason's partners in the racing syndicate, Arnie Egglersley.

'Fantastic. Absolutely excellent,' enthused Thomas.

'It's a great hobby,' said Arnie, joining the two friends. 'You should take it up, Thomas. Brilliant relaxation. A top footballer like you needs a hobby.'

Thomas thought for a moment. It wasn't the first time that someone had suggested he took up an interest outside football. His mother Elaine was always nagging on about it. Most of the other players in the Sherwood Strikers' first team had a hobby. Brad Trainor had several: he was a passionate horse rider, wind surfer, card player and gambler. Rory Betts was a brilliant guitarist as well as a computer freak. Ashleigh Coltrane was lead singer in his own reggae band. Psycho Oldie owned a pub in town – most people wouldn't call that a hobby, but Psycho did. Paul Claudel played golf almost to pro level and Cozzie Lagattello was very nearly as good. Sean Pincher was an ice skater and skipper Jamie MacLachlan, a dedicated deep-sea angler. And Jason had his racing car.

I do lots of things, thought Thomas. I run, I listen to music . . .

'Don't waste your breath, Arnie,' said Jason with a grin. 'Thomas is a couchie. He likes his home life. Mother's cooking, a bit of telly, a snooze on the sofa, maybe some clubbing in the evening, if he's not too tired. Rest of the time it's football, football, football.'

Thomas smiled. 'Maybe I'll take you up and get a racer,' he said. 'I reckon I was quicker than you and I've never driven on a track before. Call it natural talent.'

But, although he'd really enjoyed himself on the circuit and would definitely love another drive in the car, in his heart of hearts, Thomas knew he hadn't really got the bug – not like

Jason. Maybe he did stick around the house too much. Home was the office too because his mother, Elaine, was also his manager. They spent a lot of time together mapping out Thomas's deals and interests off the field. And after training and working out he didn't feel much like doing anything else. On the other hand ...

A confirmed gadget-lover, Thomas reached into his pocket and took out his iPhone. He keyed in ACTION.

1. *Check out chalet in St Lucia for Elaine.*
2. *Talk to Joss Morecombe about Japan summer tour.*
3. *Dates for Katie Moncrief!for book.*
4. *Reply tofan mail.*

With a sigh he added a fifth item.

5. *Get a hobby.*

'What's the problem?' asked Jason, watching his friend with amusement.

'Just planning my future,' replied Thomas.

'Good. Time you planned something,' said Jason amiably. He adjusted the headphones of his iPod and selected another album. 'Ready to hit the skies?'

*

	P	W	L	D	F	A	Pts
West Thames Wanderers	12	8	1	3	25	9	27
Barbican	12	6	0	6	24	10	24
Newlynn City	11	7	2	2	25	17	23
Derwent Athletic	12	6	1	5	23	20	23
Highfield Rovers	12	6	3	3	25	18	21
St James	11	6	2	3	19	14	21
Sherwood Strikers	**12**	**5**	**4**	**3**	**22**	**13**	**18**
Danebridge Forest	12	4	2	6	19	18	18
Branston Town	12	4	2	6	17	18	18
Border Town	11	4	3	4	15	15	16
Fenland Rangers	12	4	4	4	17	18	16
Mersey United	11	5	6	0	21	22	15
White Hart United	12	3	4	5	15	16	14
Kingstown Academy	12	3	5	4	18	20	13
Wierdale Harriers	12	2	6	4	18	24	10
Mersey City	11	2	5	4	15	24	10
Southdown United	11	1	4	6	18	23	9
Wednesfield Royals	12	2	7	3	13	21	9
Alexandra Park	12	1	10	1	10	22	4
Wyvern Vale	12	0	9	3	9	26	3

Sherwood Strikers' dramatic climb up the league table, after their dismal start to the season, was the talk of all the sports columns. Four stunning victories on the trot had established them as the form team in the country and the Reds were now seventh in the table although still nine points off the leaders, West Thames

Wanderers. The change in their fortune was inexplicable. For the first few games they couldn't get a result, even against the poorest opposition; now they were beating the best with some ease. As Paul Claudel, their £25 million star striker from France put it, in his unique way, 'The eagle is beautiful only when he flies in the mountains with his open wings.' Which quite probably meant the same as Psycho Oldie when he said, 'At last we're playing like a team instead of like 11 show ponies.'

Ahead lay the second leg of their UEFA Cup match away to Real Madrid. Strikers had taken a commanding 3-1 lead in the first game and they were just about favourites to knock out the mighty Spanish team, although everyone knew that, having scored the away goal, the Spanish side was capable of reversing. Strikers' advantage. In the Premier League there were tough games looming against current leaders West Thames Wanderers, and Mersey United. And the first round of the FA Cup was approaching too. Even Strikers' big squad was,stretched to the limits at the moment as the fixtures piled up and the injuries took their toll. Ashleigh Coltrane had a broken leg and would be out for most of the season; Little Mac McEwan had gone down with a mystery virus; and the lynch pin of the defence,

Brad Trainor, had torn a knee ligament.

Some of the other players were feeling the strain too. 'Psycho' Oldie had had little match practice recently because of suspension. He too had done a knee slightly in training and it was heavily bandaged. Sean Pincher had a suspect shoulder and Cosimo Lagattello's back was getting a lot of treatment on the physio's table for various aches and pains, although it was well known that 'Pasta' was a complete hypochondriac.

Finally there was Drew Stilton. Drew's discipline record had reached a low ebb, even by his low standards. In spite of manager Joss Morecombe's mixture of friendly chats and open threats, he was constantly missing training or turning up so late that it was hardly worth getting changed. Everyone knew that Drew's problem was the booze – and probably drugs, too – or so Thomas thought. Drew and Thomas had settled for being enemies from their first days at Trent Park. Every now and again war broke out between them; the last time had been during the World Cup campaign when Drew had been disciplined and finally sent home in the middle of the competition. It amazed Thomas that Joss Morecombe hadn't sacked him after that but the Strikers manager remained resolute that he would persevere with his wayward young front runner. However, when Thomas was playing well and getting rave notices in the newspapers, Drew went into a sulky decline. Drew had not been seen by the players for some days and rumours were flying around that he'd checked into a rehabilitation centre for his drinking problems. Joss Morecombe appeared unconcerned about his absence, which suggested the manager was well aware of Drew's whereabouts.

To offset the shortage of players Joss Morecombe was back in the transfer market seeking new talent. The press were sure that he was about to sign Walter Andersson, the promising 19-year-old defender from Helsingborg, and there were rumours that he was looking for a midfielder, too.

But, for all the problems, confidence was high in the Strikers' ranks and Thomas had never enjoyed his football more. As usual, he was thinking about football when he returned home after his afternoon on the racing circuit and found a little red Fiat parked in the drive. Its owner was the last person Thomas could ever have expected to see. In front of him, in his own living room, large as life, stood his dad. Sandy Cameron had walked out on his family when Richie was born, nearly 13 years ago. He'd turned up 'again once, some years later, stayed for a few weeks and then disappeared again, seemingly for good. Since then they had heard nothing from him. Not even a birthday or Christmas card. Thomas and Richie had adopted their mother's surname and Elaine never mentioned their father. The boys didn't talk about him much either.

Thomas pretended that he'd forgotten his father existed, although he thought about him quite a lot – wondering where he was, what he was doing. So it was a huge shock to see the instantly recognisable, big, burly figure with thinning grey hair and a charming smile, sitting chatting to Elaine as if he'd never been away. Sandy didn't even seem to have aged much. He was talking as if he'd just popped out to the pub and come back again, rather than having been away for all those years. Elaine, however, looked strained, uncomfortable and irritable. Richie was there too, staring in fascination at his father.

'In case you don't remember him, Thomas, this is your father,' said Elaine, her voice cold and full of sarcasm.

'I've been telling your brother what a lousy dad I've been,' said Sandy shaking Thomas by the hand. 'Worse than lousy. And I've come to say sorry.'

'A bit late for sorry, isn't it?' said Elaine.

Sandy ignored her and turned to Thomas again. 'I've always followed your career, son. I watch all your games and I've videoed most of them and I've got books full of newspaper cuttings ... You could say I'm your greatest fan. You've made me very proud.'

Big deal, thought Thomas. You could have picked up the phone or written to tell me how proud you were, instead of nothing for years and years.

'I was too ashamed before to tell you how I felt,' continued Sandy. 'But now things are different. I've come to terms with all that.'

'How?' Thomas asked. He realised it was the first word he'd addressed to his father.

'I've made a new start. There are things in my past I'm not proud of. But it's different now. I've seen the light,' said Sandy.

'Well we don't need you around here,' said Elaine. 'We've managed very nicely without you. And we'll continue to manage.'

'I'm not asking for much, Elaine,' said Sandy. 'Now that I've found the right path I need your forgiveness for my mistakes. I want to put things right if I can.'

'So you're staying, are you?'

'Yes, I've taken a little flat in town – near the football ground. You must all come and see it. And I've got a ticket for your next match at home, son. Against Mersey United a week on Saturday, isn't it?'

'Will you come and watch me play, too?' asked Richie.

'Of course I will. Of course I will, son,' said Sandy Cameron, smiling benignly.

'What's he after?' asked Thomas, when his father had left.

'I don't know,' replied Elaine. 'All this talk of conversion and right paths and seeing the light makes me very suspicious. The only time your father saw the light was through the bottom of a glass just before he fell over.'

'Why are you both being so cynical?' asked Richie. 'He's my dad. Why shouldn't he be inter-ested in what we're doing?'

'Why wasn't he interested before?' said Thomas.

'But he's different now.'

'Leopards don't change their spots,' said Elaine.

'You're wrong. I liked him,' said Richie. 'He says he's changed. At least give him a chance. It can't hurt.'

Thomas looked at Elaine. She smiled, a little sadly. 'It always hurts,' she said.

2

SPANISH LIGHTS

A win against the league leaders, West Thames Wanderers, was just the result Strikers needed before their game in Madrid. And it was a good win: 2–0. Thomas had a hand in both the goals. The second was spectacular – a floated free kick found Thomas free on the wing and he raced to the by-line and crossed inch perfect to Franco Jordan on the far post whose forceful header found the back of the net.

Sean Pincher didn't play in the Wanderers game; his shoulder was still giving him trouble and he pulled out of the trip to Madrid, too. So Thomas's friend Rory Betts, the young USA keeper, got a rare chance to play in the first team. Dean Oldie was back in defence after suspension – which was just as well in the absence of the influential Brad Trainor. The 16 players who travelled to Madrid were expecting a hard game and the manager went for an opportunistic 4–5–1 formation with the accent on defence but the wingers and Paul Claudel looking for the all-important away goal on the break.

Rory Betts

Jason Le Braz   **Dean Oldie**   **Tarquin Kelly**   **Ben El Harra**

Curtis Cropper   **Franco Jordan**   **Petr Pahler**

Jamie MacLachlan (capt)   **Thomas Headley**

Paul Claudel

Reserves: Ben Stockley (goal), Ezal Delmonty, Cosimo Lagatello, Haile Reifer.

Real Madrid attacked from the kick-off, spurred on by their amazing crowd. Thomas had played in Italy and Turkey but he had never witnessed anything to match the Spanish arena for sight or sound. They had brought fireworks and firecrackers and bass drums and every other imaginable musical instrument to the game. A giant banner of eleven Spanish onions, each bearing a picture of one of the players in the Madrid team, was unfurled on one side of the ground; it ran almost half the length of the pitch. As proceedings began an enormous fire was lit behind the Madrid goal. Back home the police and stewards would have moved in, but here no one seemed to turn a hair. The noise was tremendous. Twice in the opening minutes the game continued long after the ref's whistle sounded, because none of the players had heard a thing.

The Madrid team were electrified by their fans. For the first five minutes not a single Strikers player, except Rory Betts in goal, got a touch of the ball. Rory, however, had plenty to do. First he tipped over a flashing header from a corner. Then he punched out the cross from the right and parried a cracking volley and finally he picked the ball out of the back of his net, having failed to get even close to an unbelievable strike from 25 yards by the great Brazilian, Jose Santana.

The Real Madrid midfield which included Han Krum the Bulgarian captain and the two stars of the Spanish national side, Jaume Serra and Santiago Santa Maria Ruiz, were simply running the show and the Sherwood players seemed totally out-classed. But slowly the red shirts fought back. Led by the tenacity of skipper Jamie MacLachlan, they began to tackle their way into the game. Big Mac was everywhere. He won the ball on his own goal line, passed to Petr Pahler, took the return pass out on the wing, ran thirty yards and crossed the full length of the pitch to Thomas on the left. Thomas went outside his marker and centred to Franco Jordan whose first-time strike was only parried by the keeper. And Big Mac was there to battle for the ball on the rebound. He even managed to get his shot on target, but unfortunately it was straight at the goalkeeper.

By half time Strikers were back in contention and, if anything, they had had the most posses-sion over the full 45 minutes. But the whole team was well aware that, with away goals counting double, Madrid needed only one more score to go ahead over the two legs.

'I'm really proud of the way you weathered that storm,' said Joss Morecombe to his players in the interval. 'I can't think of another team in Europe that wouldn't have buckled under that battering. For a moment I thought we were going to be out-classed – but you checked them. It took real character and I can't tell you how important it is for a team to show character when they're under the cosh. Now it's your turn to put them under pressure.'

'Haw ya ken fine well we'll need ta poot a goal

past them an' we're gauny get it. No danger,' said Big Mac, clenching his fists in determination.

'Mac's right,' said Joss who had the uncanny knack of understanding the captain when hardly anyone else had picked up a word of what he was talking about. 'We've got to press forward more, keep closing them down in midfield and release the wingers in turn. First Thomas plays up with Paul and then Big Mac. But I want you to defend in numbers. Don't leave yourselves stretched at the back, because Santana will punish you if you do.'

'Nae worries, Boss. We'll tank 'em in the next hauf,' said the skipper.

The second half began with Strikers competing hard and winning more than their share of the 50–50 balls. Then Curtis Cropper got an ankle injury and Cozzie Lagattello came on in his place. Immediately the Sicilian carved his name on the game with a perfect throughball to Claudel who shuffled past his marker and hit the post with a cracking left foot drive.

Thomas and Petr Pahler were beginning to threaten down the left too, and Pahler's speed and strength took him past two defenders, his low, forceful shot slipping just wide of an upright. But at the other end Madrid were still dangerous and Ruiz combined with Santana to create the best chance of the half. The Brazilian's powerful shot was on target until Rory Betts tipped it round the post.

Twenty minutes from the end Thomas cut inside and took a diagonal pass from Cosimo. He worked a one-two with Claudel and fired in a shot from 25 yards. The ball struck the post but the rebound fell perfectly for Thomas who had continued his run on goal. He tucked the ball away under the diving keeper.

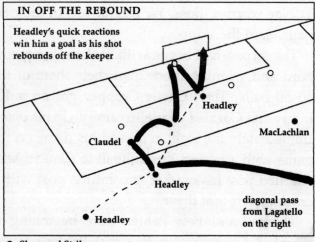

That gave the Reds a two-goal cushion and their little band of supporters – maybe five thousand of them – began their celebrations, a touch early it transpired. Santana dragged Madrid back into the game with a dazzling solo run, beating five defenders and slamming his shot past an amazed Rory Betts in the Sherwood goal. But, as both teams were roared on by the fans and the firecrackers threatened to blow the stadium apart, Thomas broke free again down the left and whipped in a pass behind the defence. As he hit the ball he felt a stabbing pain at the back of his thigh. The keeper came out to punch the cross away and missed it completely. Behind him Paul Claudel headed calmly into an empty net.

Two–two. And the ref's whistle blew before Madrid could threaten again. Joss Morecombe was as happy as a schoolboy. He ran round shaking hands and hugging every member of his team. This was the trophy Joss wanted more than any other, there was no doubt about that. And Joss knew that this year they were in with a real chance. After all, they had defeated the great Real Madrid 5–3 on aggregate. No team. in the world could have hoped to do better. When the manager reached Thomas he noticed that he was limping and wincing with pain.

'What is it, lad?'

'My hammy. I think I've torn it.'

'The same one you injured last season.'

'Yeah,' said Thomas gloomily. His injury twelve months ago had cost him nearly a dozen games out of the first team. And this didn't feel at all good. The last thing he wanted at this stage in his career was an extended stretch on the sick list. Rory and Jason helped him limp off the pitch to join the celebrations in the dressing room. Psycho and Tarquin Kelly were working their way though the Strikers' song book and no one paid much attention to Thomas.

'You light up my senses
Like a greasy chip butty
Oh Sherwood Strikers
Come thrill me again.
You'll not find our equals
Come cheer the Red men
La la la la la – laaaaa la
La la la la laa la la – OOOOAARGHFFFFF!'

And so began a night of riotous celebration in Madrid which Thomas missed out on because he was taken back to his hotel room by taxi and, after a short medical inspection of his hamstring, he spent the rest of the evening in his room with ice packs strapped to his thigh.

*

Katie Moncrieff was having coffee with Elaine when Thomas arrived home by taxi from the airport next morning. Katie was a writer for the Mirror and one of the few good football journalists. She had been a good friend to Thomas since his arrival at the Premier League side and there wasn't much Katie didn't know about football and about Strikers in particular. Now she was busy ghostwriting books for two of the Strikers' players. The first was a sort of season-in-the-life of the Premier League diary by Paul Claudel; the other was Thomas's World Cup story. Thomas and Katie had already had one session together planning the book and Katie had given Thomas a little tape recorder and told him to relate the story of the month of the World Cup in his own words. So far he'd done about ten minutes – he found it really hard to sit down and concentrate and he was also very nervous about telling stories which would embarrass or offend other players in the club.

'Sorry about the injury,' said Katie. 'How bad is it?'

'The doc says I'm out for two or three weeks. Could be worse.'

'Well at least that will give you some time to work on the book. How are you getting on with it?'

Thomas shrugged and, as Katie looked for an explanation, he said, 'You see I'm not sure what to include. All the good stories are a bit private. I mean, my mates in the team have told me loads of stuff but they don't expect me to put it all in a book, do they?'

'You should let me worry about that. Tell me everything you want and we'll decide together whether it goes into the book or not.'

'And I'll have a good read of it too before it gets published,' said Elaine warily.

'But what about Drew?' asked Thomas. 'Everyone knows there's trouble between us. But he was part of the squad until he got slung out. I've got to put something in about him. But if I say what I think he'll sue me.'

'Yes I can see that might be a problem,' said Katie. 'It won't be easy to tell the story about him coming in drunk and trying to deck you in the team hotel.'

'You won't even mention it,' said Elaine. 'That one never got out, thank goodness. Imagine what the press would make of it. And you're right about him suing us – Arun Canin will call in the lawyers if you blink at him.' Arun Canin was

Drew's unscrupulous manager and Thomas and Elaine already had cause to be wary of his methods, having come close to losing a lot of money in a shady Canin restaurant venture.

'Don't worry, Thomas. Get it down on the tape and we'll try and work it out later,' said Katie to Thomas. 'You know you can trust me.' 'Okay,' said Thomas rather gloomily. 'Like you say, I'll have plenty of time on my hands over the next couple of weeks.'

'Then maybe you'll have time to answer some of your fan letters,' said Elaine. 'There are piles of them in the office. And I want you to talk to your brother about his dad. The old devil's asked him to move into his flat for a few days. If he gets Richie under his thumb there's no telling what will happen. I don't want him to go but if I say no, it'll just make him more determined. Both of my sons are a bit stubborn I'm afraid.' Katie smiled. 'Sounds as if you might be busier than you thought,' she said to Thomas. 'But if you've got any spare time you can always come and watch me rock climbing.'

'Rock climbing?'

'Yes, it's my new hobby. There's a brilliant new indoor place at Craggy Park. I'm already climbing some of the serious walls and I can't wait to get back to Scotland and try the real thing. It's great relaxation – you should have a go when you're fit again.'

'Sound a bit dangerous to me,' said Thomas.

'Funny. That's what I thought you'd say, Thomas,' said Katie with a smile.

3
THE RIVALS

As the music faded in the DJ's voice signed off at the end of his show. 'But stay tuned, folks, 'cos right after the break we have a sensational new Radio Sherwood Metro feature for you, with the main man who knows all the secrets of the stars – Barney Haggard!'

'Why are we listening to this junk?' asked Thomas leaning forward to switch off his car radio. He and Jason le Braz were on their way to Trent Park in Thomas's Saab convertible for the official opening of the club's new executive wing.

'Wait,' said Jason. 'I think you'll want to hear Barney's special guest.'

The extra smarmy tones of the world's most slimy radio presenter took over the air waves. 'Yes, folks, it's me, Barney Haggard, with a brand new show. And the focus is everybody's favourite sport, yes, that's right, footie. Only this one is different. It isn't about the action on the field, it's the action off the field. I'll be looking at what's new and exciting in the lives of the top players. I'll be telling you the things you want to know, and some things we're not supposed to know, too. And today my special guest is a star player who's had his ups and downs, but there's no doubt that he and his team are on cracking form right now. So don't go away – he'll be with you after the break.'

'You know who it is, don't you?' said Thomas suspiciously.

Jason grinned. 'Maybe. But I can hardly hear what he's saying on this crap sound system of yours. You want to get yourself a Stereolab like mine. It's brilliant. Wall to wall sound – makes the Audi sound like you've got a live band playing in the back seat.'

'Who is it, you idiot?'

'You'll find out soon enough. I'll give you a clue, though. He's one of your favourite players.'

'A Strikers player?'

'Yep.'

As the ads ended Barney Haggard introduced his guest. 'He's a star of Sherwood Strikers and England. He's one of the most talented players in the country. And from what I've learned he's not at all shy about his talent. He's the Reds' number 11. He's . . .'

'Oh no!' Thomas almost put his head in his hands and then he remembered he was driving through heavy traffic.

'. . . Drew Stilton. Well, Drew, we've got a lot to ask you about today. How did you feel when you were kicked out of the World Cup squad, for instance? And what about the booze? Have you kicked it, mate? But first I'd like to talk about Strikers and some of the guys in the team.'

'Guess what Drew's up to?' said Jason. 'He's had one game back in the squad after his "holiday" at the drying out farm, scored a couple of goals and now we're all going to hear about it.'

'We all know Strikers are a great team,' continued Barney Haggard, 'but what would you do to make them even better?'

'Well,' began Drew. 'I'd say we've still got a few weaknesses – particularly in midfield. The front runners like me don't get enough service most of the time. Mind you, it's better now that Petr Pahler is playing on the left.'

'Thomas Headley's out with an injury right now, isn't he? Are you saying you don't like playing with him? I mean it's common knowledge that you two don't get on, isn't it?'

'You don't have to like someone to play together,' said Drew, slyly.

'So you'd like to see him back in the team?'

'I didn't say that. I think we're showing more style than we've done all season. It might be a coincidence that Headley's out of the team at the moment. Or it might be something else.'

'Do you blame him for you being slung out of the England side by Jacky Dooley?'

'Yeah. He had a lot to do with it.'

'And I hear he's writing a book about his World Cup adventures. What do you think he'll say about you?'

'I don't give a damn what he says. I just know I'm a better player than Headley and that's enough for me.'

Thomas reached out and killed the radio. 'If you haven't had enough of this, I have.'

'You've got to laugh,' said Jason. 'The guy's a nutter. He's living in a world of make believe.'

'It doesn't make me laugh,' said Thomas. 'If Drew's out to get me, I promise you, I'm going to hammer him first.'

'You take care, mate. If you write anything about him in that book of yours, Arun Canin is just the type to give you a lot of grief. And that won't help your career at Strikers.'

Thomas pulled into the Trent Park players'

car park and got out of the car. His hamstring was still painful, and he was not looking forward to his session with the physio later in the day. If he didn't get a decent report he would be out for weeks. He was hoping for a run out with the reserves on Saturday with, maybe, an outside chance of getting back into the first team the following week. He hated being injured because it just reminded him that he lived for football. While he was playing it was fine, but when he stopped he realised how important the game was to him. If he had to give up football he would die. And he hated mooching around the house – particularly at the moment when things were anything but easy. Richie had moved out for a few days to stay with his dad and Elaine was concerned that it would become a permanent arrangement. She was genuinely worried that their father would be a bad influence on him. Thomas wasn't best pleased about it either. He liked having Richie around, although he could be a pest at times, and without him Thomas had to take the full brunt of Elaine's moaning. All in all he was beginning to wish Sandy Cameron had never showed up at all.

Thomas and Jason joined all the other players and their agents who were on duty for the function to open the new executive suite. The building had gone up amazingly quickly and it was pretty stylish. There was a very smart new players' lounge with loads of facilities such as saunas and massage rooms; a modern press room wired up with every kind of electronic link-up imaginable; and the pride and joy of Monty Windsor, the club's chairman, a brand new Trophy Room.

The guests were mostly bigwigs from the town and wealthy friends of the Sherwood Strikers board. The name of the game was sponsorship and, of course, the new complex had a silly name to show the world that someone had spent a lot of money on it. It was called the Henry Flashman Complex; Psycho Oldie immediately renamed it Flash Harry's Hotel. All the players had been asked to turn up and all of them were there except Drew Stilton. Most of the agents had come too, including Elaine, and Thomas noticed Drew's slimy operator, Arun Canin, networking his way round the room. A sprinkling of journalists had been asked along, mostly local newspaper editors, and the TV cameras were filming it for the regional news. Katie Moncrieff was the only national sports writer on view.

'What are you doing here?' Jason asked her. 'This is not much of a news story for you.'

'Oh, I'm following Paul Claudel about for the "Diary" and Pete Frame wants me to write a piece about the new facilities for Saturday's programme and the Strikers' website.'

'You're becoming the official Strikers scribe, aren't you?' said Jason.

'So I need the money,' said Katie with a shrug.

'People are going to think you're biased,' teased Jason. 'But I'm not complaining, it's good to have a journalist on our side for a change. How are you getting on with Tommy's bestseller?'

'Okay,' Katie smiled at Thomas. 'But it'd be a lot quicker if he'd do his homework. Have you finished recording those tapes yet, Thomas?'

'Not quite,' Thomas lied. In fact, he'd done nothing. Somehow he couldn't get his head round it. 'I'll do it at the weekend. I've got plenty of time.'

Thomas usually enjoyed parties, even official ones like this, but today he was finding it hard to relax. Maybe it was the injury that was bothering him, or that stupid Radio Sherwood interview. None of the other players had heard it but Psycho said he was going to get a tape of it so that he could enjoy listening to Cheesy making a prat of himself.

Monty Windsor made a very boring speech about getting some silverware this season for his Trophy Room to add to the fine display of cups and shields from previous decades and, of course, last season's FACup. After the formalities Joss Morecombe came over to have a word with Thomas. 'How's the leg?' he asked.

'Okay,' said Thomas. 'I'm up for the Reserves game on Saturday.'

'Hmmm, we'll see what the physios and the Doc have to say about that.' Joss Morecombe's eyes bored into him. 'I'd sooner you missed a few games than wrecked yourself for the rest of the season.'

'But ...' began Thomas but his protests were cut short as Joss was dragged away by Pete Frame, the Strikers' PR supremo, who wanted the manager for yet another interview.

Strikers' chief physiotherapist, Clare Harrison, came from Yorkshire and like a lot of Yorkshire folk she didn't mince her words. 'That leg won't stand up to ten minutes of Premier League football, let alone 90.' Thomas's session was taking place in the old physio room which was a temporary building, due for demolition next week. It was about time – the floor creaked, the couches wobbled and the temperature was either tropical or freezing. Today it was hot and the sweat was pouring off Thomas as Clare went to work on his leg.

'What about a run out with the Reserves on Saturday? Can't you do something to get me a game?' he moaned.

She told him to flex his hamstring and applied some heat treatment along the ligament. 'There's nothing I or anyone else can do that would make you fit to play on Saturday. Rest's the only answer for this leg. But if you do as you're told and rest it, you might be able to come on for a short spell the following week. For the Reserves, mind – not the first team.'

After the pummelling Clare gave him Thomas felt he wouldn't walk for a month and he hobbled disconsolately back to the new players' suite. The guests had all gone; the rooms were empty. Or almost empty – a couple of waitresses were gathering up glasses and giggling together.

'Look,' whispered one. 'It's Deadly Headley!'

'Oooh!' said the other.

Thomas recognised them: Milly Valentini and Lercher Robson, constant fans of the Reds. Milly was the short, chatty one, Lercher, tall, gangly and giggly.

'How did you two get in here?' he asked.

'We were hired as waitresses, weren't we, Lerch,' said Milly proudly. 'The caterers needed extra staff and they took us on. We'd have done it for free but we're getting paid too. How's your leg? When are you going to play again?'

'Soon. Have you seen any of the other players?'

'I spoke to Paul Claudel,' giggled Lercher. 'I said, "Bonjour, Claudo".'

'What about Jason?' asked Thomas.

'He's in the gym getting hot and sweaty,' said Milly. Lercher giggled again.

Jason had finished his workout in the new gym and had changed back into his suit. He was hunting round the changing room for something.

'I put my watch down here, with my gear, and it's gone,' he said. 'It was my Rolex. You know, the one I got from the sponsors when I scored in the Cup semi-final. It was inscribed with my name.'

Thomas remembered that Monty Windsor, the Strikers' chairman, had presented a Rolex Oyster watch to each of the three players who had scored in that unforgettable game against St James.

'It must be around somewhere.'

'I reckon someone's nicked it,' said Jason.

'Then we'd better tell the boss or Pete Frame.'

When the two friends turned up at Joss Morecombe's office they found the pokey little room was packed with other people also reporting strange disappearances which had all taken place during or just after the reception. Len Dallal claimed that three presentation footballs, signed by all the first team for a charity raffle, had vanished. Sean Pincher had lost his World Cup medal from his locker. And several silver trophies and framed photographs were missing from the new Trophy Room.

'Lucky the FA Cup's in the bank vault,' said Joss Morecombe. 'Or we'd have lost that too. It looks to me as if we've had a professional tea leaf wandering amongst our guests this afternoon.'

'It might have been a gang working together,' suggested Pete Frame.

'Certainly someone who knew his way around,' added Joss. 'The thefts took place over a wide area. Even I can't find my way through the new complex yet.'

'The security guards have got a full list of all the guests and the catering staff,' said Pete Frame. 'I wouldn't have thought many of the people here today needed to steal a watch or a signed football. They were all pretty well-heeled.'

'Well I'm afraid we're going to have to call the police,' said Joss. 'And that most likely means the press will be involved. So much for our little PR stunt. We'll get bags of publicity all right – but not the sort we wanted.'

4

THE WAITING GAME

Thomas stared at his Strikers programme. He was sitting in the Trent Park stand immediately behind the reserves bench. It was the third round of the FA Cup, the first for the Premiership sides, and Strikers had been drawn at home against Second Division Dawlston Albion.

The Reds' recordover the past ten days should have made pleasant reading for Thomas. Two handsome wins, one against the league leaders, seven goals and Strikers were now fourth in the table. But the bad news was that Drew Stilton had scored four of the seven goals – and he hadn't stopped talking about them ever since. If I hear about that brilliant overhead kick into the top corner of the net again, 'thought Thomas, I shall go and lie down under a bus. He'd not spoken to Drew since the infamous interview on the Barney Haggard show but all the other players were talking about it. After playing the tape to the whole team Psycho thought it was a huge laugh and told Thomas to relax. But Rory Betts said Drew had overstepped the mark and so did Petr Pahler who was always surprised by the things that appeared in the tabloids and on the radio in England. He was used to more respectful treatment from the media in his country.

There was one further incident involving Drew Stilton which raised a few eyebrows. Before training he ostentatiously gathered together all his gear, placed it in his locker, and locked it. Usually the players left their stuff lying around the dressing room. 'How do we know that the thief isn't one of the team?' he asked when he saw his team-mates watching him.

'Because I don't reckon any of us would want to run a stall at a car boot sale,' said Psycho.

'Act your age, Cheesy. Why would anyone here want to nick stuff from his mates?' asked Jason.

Drew shrugged and said no more but his look gave the impression that he had his suspicions.

As the teams ran out on to the pitch Thomas looked down at his programme again. There it was in print.

St James United 1
Campbell (34)

Sherwood Strikers 3
Stilton (12, 67)
Claudel (89)

Sherwood Strikers 4
Stilton (5, 80) MacLachlan (82)
Lagattello (85)

Mersey United 1
Trinder (46)

	P	W	L	D	F	A	Pts
West Thames Wanderers	15	9	2	4	31	11	31
Barbican	14	7	0	7	25	10	28
Newlynn City	14	8	2	4	28	19	28
Sherwood Strikers	**15**	**8**	**4**	**3**	**31**	**15**	**27**
Highfield Rovers	15	7	5	3	27	21	24
Derwent Athletic	15	6	3	6	25	26	24
Danebridge Forest	14	5	2	7	22	19	22
St James	14	6	4	4	20	19	22
Branston Town	15	5	3	7	19	20	22
White Hart United	15	5	4	6	19	16	21
Fenland Rangers	14	5	4	5	20	19	20
Mersey United	14	6	7	1	23	27	19
Border Town	15	4	5	6	18	23	18
Kingstown Academy	15	4	6	5	23	23	17
Mersey City	15	4	6	5	18	23	17
Wierdale Harriers	14	3	6	5	20	24	14
Wednesfield Royals	14	3	7	4	15	24	13
Southdown United	14	1	5	8	20	27	11
Alexandra Park	14	1	11	2	10	23	5
Wyvern Vale	15	0	11	4	9	33	4

Thomas looked at Joss Morecombe's programme notes. His words about Drew Stilton caught his eye:

'Drew's return to form is just the bonus we need at the moment with so many players on the injury list. He's capable of the spectacular goal or the brilliant run through a defence. But what I like about his game right now is that he is learning to read the big picture. His passing and running off the ball have improved immeasurably.'

What a load of old cobblers, thought Thomas. Joss Morecombe ought to know better than to write that sort of stuff about Drew; he's got a big enough head already. But Thomas knew in his heart that Drew was playing well and he couldn't blame the manager for trying to coax more excellent performances out of him.

The real news about Drew was that since his return from three weeks in a rehab centre in the Lake District to tackle his drinking problem he'd been even more insufferable than usual. Somehow Joss had managed to keep most of the story about Drew's drinking problems away from the press even though Drew's manager, Arun Canin, was hardly proving helpful in this respect. Canin's view was that any publicity was good publicity. There were rumours flying around that the boss had handed out yet another final warning to Drew and his manager after the Radio Sherwood interview. Drew had had more final warnings than first team appearances for Strikers and it wasn't just Thomas who thought that the manager was giving him an easy ride.

As for Joss's team selection for the Cup game, it bore little resemblance to the victorious side which had played in Madrid.

Sean Pincher

Jason Le Braz   Dean Oldie   Tarquin Kelly   Walter Andersson

Cosimo Lagattello   Jamie MacLachlan   Francisco Panto-Gomes   Petr Pahler

Drew Stilton   Paul Claudel

Walter Andersson, the Reds' new signing from Sweden, had been drafted .into the team in his first week. There were two other new faces on the bench, too: Jimmy Baino from Sultan Palace who had joined Strikers for £5.6 million to strengthen the midfield and the winger, Vijay Goonasekera, who was on loan for two months from Mersey City to cover for the injuries to Ashleigh Coltrane and Lanny McEwan. Little Mac's virus was still puzzling the medics. He looked okay but kept complaining of complete lack of energy and weakness in his legs.

The game began with an astonishing goal inside the first minute. Unfortunately for Thomas it was scored by Drew Stilton. Pahler provided a diagonal ball from the left and Stilton took it on his chest, looped the ball back over his head with his right foot, turned his marker and struck a rasping drive on the half-volley with his left that gave the Dawlston keeper no chance.

Drew pulled his shirt over his head, ran to the corner flag and then turned to receive the congratulations of his team-mates before bowing theatrically to the fans. It was a typical Stilton performance – completely over the top and self-serving – or so Thomas thought.

Two minutes later Drew added to the scoreline with a sharp header and by half time Strikers led 4–0 and the game was as good as over.

Len Dallal, Strikers' chief coach who was sitting in front of Thomas, turned round. 'Your mate Stilton's having another goodish game,' he said. Len was not one for over-statement. 'Goodish' was as enthusiastic as he got.

'He's no mate of mine,' muttered Thomas.

'Don't worry, lad. I'm not too fond of the cocky little beggar, either. But he's a useful footballer when he puts his mind to it. How's that injury of yours coming along?'

'Not bad. I'm playing in the Reserves next Saturday to test it out. And if there's no reaction I should be back the following week.'

'We'll have to see how you shape up in training next week. But make sure you pull out all the stops in the Reserves game. The Gaffer isn't one to disturb a successful team when it's on a winning run. You'll need to be in sparky form to catch his eye and force your way back – England star or no.'

Thomas grinned. He knew old Doolally was right. It wasn't just Drew who was playing well. Petr Pahler and Cisco Panto-Gomes had been showing some real class too. And Pasta Lagattello was enjoying his best spell of form at the club. At times today his passing and timing had been breathtaking.

In the second half Drew scored twice more to bring his tally for the game to four and an impressive total of eight goals in three games since his return to the team. Thomas was sure that he saw Drew waving the match ball in his direction with a sly look of triumph as he jogged off at the end of the game to the cheers of the crowd. Sherwood ran out 7–1 winners.

Just to rub salt in the wounds, Thomas saw Drew's manager, Arun Canin, arranging interviews with a bunch of enthusiastic journalists as he passed the press box on his way out. Katie was one of them. She walked over to talk to Thomas.

'This is the bit of my job that I don't much like,' she said. 'Talking to shady agents like Arun Canin.'

'Then why do you do it? Drew's not supposed to be talking to the press anyway.'

'What am I to do about that? Drew's hot news right now and Joss Morecombe knows it. If I miss out on the story and the pictures my editor will be deeply unimpressed.'

'I don't know what all the fuss is about. He had a good enough game, but the opposition weren't much, were they?' said Thomas grudgingly.

'I don't want to talk about Drew Stilton. It's bad enough having to write about him. How's the leg?'

'Better. I'm playing for the Reserves next week.'

'Fancy some rock climbing to tone you up?'

'Yeah. Why not.'

'Wednesday morning, then. And maybe I can check a few facts for the book afterwards. I've written the first four chapters. That takes it up to the United States game. I'd forgotten that Drew got the equalizer in that one. If he hadn't scored England would have been out of the tournament.'

'It's supposed to be my book – not Drew Stilton's,' said Thomas sulkily.

'But I've got to get the facts straight.'

'Then you can tell everyone how he got paralytic and punched me in the head afterwards and was chucked out of the team hotel,' said Thomas.

Katie looked at him calmly. 'I've been thinking about how we're going to handle that one. I think we should leave it out entirely. If we tell the whole story things are going to get really nasty between you and Drew.'

'They couldn't get much worse. And people should be told the truth.'

'But the press will get hold of it and twist it and you might regret dragging the whole thing up again.'

'I'll take the risk,' said Thomas.

'Any news on the Trent Park thief?' asked Katie, to change the subject.

'The police have been interviewing people but I don't think they've got a clue.'

'It's a strange one. I don't think it's an ordinary burglary.'

'I know what you mean – the way a few things were taken from one place and a few from another. I mean they took Jason's watch but left his money. And they only took five cups from the Trophy Room when they could have nicked the lot.'

'Claudo thinks it's a practical joke.'

'Claudo?' mimicked Thomas with a smile.

'Paul's an interesting guy you know,' said Katie, ignoring him. 'He's a very keen wildlife photographer and he also writes poetry.'

'You're not going to put his poetry in the book, are you?' asked Thomas with a chuckle.

'And why not? I might use some of his photographs too. They're very good.'

'I thought it was supposed to be a football book. I don't think too many Reds supporters are interested in French poems and pictures of tawny owls.'

'He writes in English, too.'

'Oh really.' Thomas suddenly realised that he was getting rather bored with the direction the conversation was taking and he was relieved to see his little brother Richie coming towards them.

'Guess who got a hat trick this morning?' said

Richie. His broad smile left no one in any doubt about the answer.

'Congratulations,' said Katie.

'Yeah, we beat St James 5–2. Dad says it was the most exciting game he's ever watched. He's sorry he missed you at the reception on Thursday, by the way, Tommy.'

'I didn't know he was there,' said Thomas.

'Yeah, he got an invitation from one of the directors. But I think he arrived late. Dad's really good at making new friends, you know. He gets loads of invites all over the place.'

'Do you like it – living at his flat?' asked Katie.

'You bet,' said Richie. 'He lets me do anything I like without moaning on at me about school work like Elaine does. And he drives me to all the Highfield Juniors games too.'

'Does that mean you're not doing any home-work?' asked Thomas in a serious sort of voice that made him feel a bit hypocritical.

' 'Course I am. But I'm having a good time with Dad, too. He wants me to stay for another week. Do you think Elaine will mind?'

'You'd better ask her,' said Thomas. But he knew the answer. Elaine would mind like hell. And yet there was nothing she could say.

5

TWIST AGAIN

'This place is just too quiet without Richie around,' said Elaine. 'I want him back.'

'He'll be okay,' said Thomas.

'I wish I could feel that,' said Elaine. 'I know your father better than you do. He's up to something. I don't know what it is, but I'm sure it'll end in tears. It always does.'

Thomas couldn't decide how he felt about his dad. It was hard to believe that Sandy really cared about his sons after the way he had behaved. And yet he did appear to have made a genuine effort to change his way of life. He seemed to thoroughly enjoy spending time with him and Richie. Surely they all had to give him a chance to prove himself, Elaine included.

But Thomas could sense that Sandy's presence in Sherwood was really worrying his mother and that made it even more difficult for him, particularly as he needed to talk to her about something that had been troubling him for some time. He was beginning to think that the moment had come for him to take on a professional agent. Elaine had managed him since his start in the professional game, and she had done a great job, he knew that. Plenty of people, Joss Morecombe and Len Dallal among them, were constantly telling him how lucky he was and how much they liked working with her. She worked hard and she was well respected. But Thomas was finding it harder and harder to be managed by his mother. It didn't seem quite right somehow and when people like Drew Stilton teased him about it he got really furious. Maybe it was the idea that he was tied to her – a bit of a mummy's boy – that hit a raw nerve. There was another side to it, however. For while Elaine knew her way round Trent Park, she did not have the connections in the national and international game that some of the top agents did. How could she? She didn't have the time to travel all over the world meeting the big noises in the game. That wasn't her style, in any case.

I need a true wheeler-dealer, thought Thomas, someone to promote me as an international star. And there had been no shortage of offers from the top agents – most recently from Franco

Delaney who managed a stable of top players including Ashleigh Coltrane and Graham Deek at Highfield Rovers.

He flexed his leg and felt the twinge again in the back of his thigh. For Thomas, every Strikers game played without him was an ordeal and, lost in his gloomy thoughts, he was becoming increasingly morose and taciturn, especially with Elaine. His injury and the Sandy Cameron business were creating more and more tension between him and his mother.

The phone rang in the room that Elaine used as an office and Thomas picked it up.

'Yeah?'

'Can I speak with Elaine Headley?' said a woman's voice. 'I'm Rita, Barney Haggard's producer from Radio Sherwood.'

Thomas was about to pass the phone to Elaine but then decided to handle it himself. 'Thomas Headley here. Can I help you?'

'Yes, of course. Well perhaps you know that Barney's doing this new series called *Behind the Net*. We'd love to have you on the prog tomorrow or the day after or whenever you're free. Would that be possible?'

Thomas's first instinct was to say, 'Not on your life.' Then he thought, hold on a minute, why not? Why shouldn't I get a chance to answer all those lies and insinuations that Drew has put about?

Elaine eyed him curiously from across the desk, wondering what the call was about.

'Yes, I'll do it,' said Thomas. 'Tomorrow morning's fine. Say 11 o'clock? I'll be there.'

'What was that about?' asked Elaine as Thomas put the phone down.

'Oh nothing interesting. Just a dumb reporter,' said Thomas, getting up and leaving the room.

The Barney Haggard interview wasn't the only thing that Thomas was keeping from Elaine. Later that morning he went to see his father without telling her. Sandy's big, comfortable, furnished flat was close to the city centre. He opened the door to Thomas with an enormous smile. 'Come in, come in, son,' he said.

Richie was there in the sitting room watching a football DVD on the large-screen TV. He waved a hand at his brother but hardly took his eye off the game. Thomas noticed it was a Highfield Rovers match. He followed his father into the kitchen.

'How's Richie getting on?' he asked.

'Great. He says he loves staying here,' said Sandy. 'It's good for me, too. We've missed a lot of years, son.'

'Elaine's really upset.'

Sandy swung round from the fridge. For a second there was an ugly look on his face that Thomas didn't much like. Then quick as a flash the smile returned. 'I just want to get to know my sons. Is that some sort of crime? She's had you both all your lives, hasn't she?'

Thomas hesitated.

'Come on, Thomas. Relax. Don't worry about your mother. She'll be fine in time. I know what she's like – a bit over anxious, eh?'

Thomas nodded, feeling somehow disloyal.

'Maybe Elaine's taking too much on – what with running the house for two lads and managing you full time,' said Sandy.

Thomas said nothing.

'Just a thought,' said Sandy. 'None of my business really. But there is something I want to talk to you about. I want your opinion. You see I may be taking a job with Strikers.'

'What?'

'Yes. They're looking for a projects manager . . . to look after the new building, the Academy, mail order, the Internet – that sort of thing. I've got a wee bit of experience in that area and I was talking to Monty Windsor . . .'

'How do you know Monty?'

'I know a lot of people at Strikers. You'd be surprised.'

Thomas did his best to look pleased at the news. But he wasn't. For some reason the very last thing he wanted was for his dad to be involved with the club. 'Have you been interviewed for the job?' he asked.

'Not yet. But I've been told informally that it's mine if I want it. And I'd like to be involved in the greatest club in the world, just like my son.' He ruffled Thomas's hair.

'What does Richie think?'

'Oh,' laughed Sandy, 'he'd rather it was Highfield Rovers but I think he's pleased. It would mean I'd be staying around here in Sherwood, you see.'

'Yes, of course.'

'Now, are we going out for lunch, or not? Richie wants a three-decker at Custer's Last Stand. I hope that's okay with you.'

At lunch, Richie talked non-stop about his latest goals for Highfield Rovers and the news of his selection for the England Youth Under 14 squad. Then Thomas had another physio session. Clare Harrison gave his leg a thorough workout and told him that he was okay to play 45 minutes maximum with the Reserves on Saturday. That was enough for Thomas; he went straight from the new physio unit to Joss Morecombe's office.

The builders certainly hadn't got their hands on Joss's den - if anything it seemed more dingy and cluttered than usual.

'I can play for the Reserves on Saturday,' said Thomas.

'Who says?'

'Clare.'

'Since when did she pick the teams round here; lad?'

'But ...'

'It's only Wednesday, Thomas. You know I don't select any of the sides till Friday.'

Thomas took a deep breath. 'You know that summer tour in the Far East, Boss?'

'Yes?'

'Well, I might feel happier about putting my name down for it if you, well, like played me on ...'

Joss looked up. 'Are you trying to blackmail me, son?'

Thomas opened his mouth to speak but Joss put a hand on his shoulder. 'Listen, lad. It's a long season. We've got a big squad but we're going to need every player in it. We're in the UEFACup .and we're the FA Cup holders and I've got my eye on both those jugs this year. But if there's one thing I really care about, it's the Premier League title. We're going to snatch it from under the noses of the likes of Albert LaBarbe and Davie Kirkham. Barbican and Highfield and St James have shared the title for too long. This year it's our turn. To be in with a chance, I've got to make the most of my resources for the whole season. And I'm not daft enough to bring you back until you're 100%. Now don't waste my time, lad. Go and do some work on that leg in the gym.'

Gloomily, Thomas made his way from the executive floor to the players' lounge. He didn't feel like training; he felt more like kicking a football through somebody's window: Joss Morecombe's, his dad's, Drew Stilton's.

As he lingered for a few minutes in the players' lounge to look through the newspaper headlines from the club's press cutting file, a big hand clapped him on the shoulder.

'Hey, Tommeh? Hoo ye daein? Haws tha wee hammy?'

'Good,' said Thomas. 'I'm playing in the Reserves on Saturday . . . if the boss gives me the green light, that is. I'll go mad if I don't get back in the first team soon.'

'Haw, ya'll be back in nae time. Ah ken how yar committed tae the work ethic.'

'You bet. I've already got a new training programme to build up the strength in my leg.'

'Guid on ye,' said the skipper. He had a post-card in his hand which he kept glancing at and then looking oddly at Thomas. 'Hae ya seen one a these afore?' He handed the card to Thomas who read it.

STRIKERS SOUVENIRS
- **Genuine club trophies**
- **Club equipment**
- **Special souvenir players' medals**
Not replicas ... the real thing
Private cash sale only

There was a telephone number at the bottom.

'Where did this come from?' asked Thomas.

'They're no hard tae find.'

'What's it all about?'

'Ye tell me. Ye see, Ah gave tha mobile number a bell,' said Big Mac.

Thomas looked at the number on the card again and his eyes widened.

'But ... that's my mobile number.'

'Aye, would ya credit it? Ah wouldny be surprised if ya have a few wee messages waitin'.'

In a daze Thomas wandered over to his new locker, took out the smart card key from his wallet and opened it. If Big Mac had surprised him, what he now saw reduced him to a state of complete shock. Inside his locker were three brand-new footballs covered in signatures, some framed photographs, several silver cups, and, on the upper shelf, a gold-banded watch and a World Cup medal. As he stared in disbelief, he was dimly aware that Big Mac had come up beside him and was looking over his shoulder. One of the footballs rolled out and bounced away across the floor.

6
REVENGE

'Sufferin' ducks, Tommeh, what hae youz got mixed up in?'

Thomas stood staring at the contents of his locker and then at the football rolling away. 'I . . . I didn't . . .' he began.

'If Ah'm no' much mistaken, you've got the whole wee statch in there,' said Big Mac, taking a closer look at the contents of the locker and picking out Jason's watch for closer inspection.

'But I didn't put them there.'

'Ah'm no sayin' ya did. But it's a wee bit strange, ya have ta admit.'

'I didn't steal this stuff. I've never seen it before. I mean, of course I've seen it, but . . .'

'Ah'm no saying youz a thief, Tommeh. But there's nae use ya tryin' ta pretend there's nowt there. Wha' are ya going to say tae tha polis?'

'The police?'

'Aye. They'll need ta be telled.'

'But look,' said Thomas furiously, 'I didn't take this stuff, I didn't put it in my locker, I don't know anything about this stupid card and I'm not a thief. Someone is stitching me up – that's what it is.'

'There's nae need for you ta take the needle, laddie. Ah'm nae accusin' ya.'

'It's Drew Stilton,' said Thomas suddenly. 'It's just the stupid, brainless sort of thing he'd do.'

'Whit is it wi you and Drew Stilton? Ah'd heet ta see ya turn oot a big no-user like him. Mind, if he did this Ah'd be the fust tae gi him a toe ender.'

In the end Big Mac persuaded Thomas to collect everything up and take it along to the manager's office. Joss was in no better mood than earlier and the sight of the cups and footballs and the other stolen stuff did little to improve his day. He glared at Thomas and then phoned security and the police. Thomas was told by the head of security that he'd be required to make a statement and Joss said that he should keep his mouth shut about the whole affair until then. Thomas tried to protest his innocence and voice his suspicions about Drew Stilton but for the second time that afternoon his words were waved aside by Joss Morecambe and he was dismissed.

*

Thomas was still seething next morning when he walked into the Radio Sherwood studio and shook the clammy hand of Barney Haggard. 'Cool to see you again, Thomas,' oozed the DJ in his fake American accent. Barney looked like an android with his fixed smile and bush of black hair which suggested heavy plastic surgery, hair dye and a wig. Thomas had met him a few times before and on each occasion he'd found him creepier than the last. Why am I doing this? he thought to himself.

'I'm just going to ask you a few questions about the Sherwood Strikers happy family and the England set-up,' said Barney. 'So just sit yourself back and RE-LAX while Barney and Suzy get the mike levels adjusted for you.'

The studio was a tiny room with no natural light and glaring, bluish spotlights. Barney Haggard was sweating profusely as he fussed about with the dials on the console in front of him, snapping instructions at Suzy, the pretty production secretary who kept smiling at Thomas.

The interview was fairly boring to begin with until Barney got on to the subject of Drew Stilton's latest successes. 'You don't kinda hit it off, you two, do you?' he asked suddenly.

'Not really,' said Thomas. He wasn't in the mood to mince words about Drew. 'In fact, you could say that I think Drew Stilton is a complete waste of space at Strikers.'

'Really? Are you saying he's not a good footballer or not a good team member?'

'I'm saying he's a crap human being,' said Thomas, suddenly feeling the anger well up inside him.

'Well, there you have it, folks,' said Barney in a hushed voice into the mike. 'Thomas Headley and Drew Stilton don't seem to be the best of mates. So tell us, what exactly happened in the World Cup between the two of you, Thomas?'

'Well, you probably know that, amongst other things, Drew's got a problem with booze and stuff. And when he's had a few he becomes even more unpleasant – which, I know, is a bit difficult to believe.'

'And you saw him drunk during the World Cup at the team headquarters?'

'Several times. That's why he was kicked out. That and trying to punch my head in.'

'You had a fight?'

'Not really a fight. Drew was out of his skull and he tried to land one on me but he wasn't very accurate. Even if he'd been sober I wouldn't have been in much danger.'

As he told Barney the story of the World Cup brawl with Drew and other things about his least favourite person, a slight unease crept into Thomas's mind. Was he going too far? Should he be talking like this in a radio interview? But he didn't seem to be able to stop himself. All the anger and frustration of the past few days came pouring out. And Barney Haggard sat there like the snake he was, hissing contentedly to himself, as Thomas spilled the beans. This is going to put my show in the big time, thought Barney to himself. Every newspaper in the country will feature this one. Thomas Headley, you're a fool, but don't stop now whatever you do. And Thomas didn't stop. He talked on and on, not only criticising Drew, but also adding a few jibes about Joss's team selection for good measure.

'That was one of the best interviews I've ever done, Thomas. You were brilliant,' oozed Barney as he finally wrapped up the session.

'When does it go out?' asked Thomas.

'This one's on Saturday evening, the prime slot after the football results. And we'll repeat it on Wednesday. Be sure to tune in. What are you doing on Saturday?'

'Playing for the Reserves.'

'Good. So the leg's better, is it? Well best of luck.'

Whatever Thomas's feelings were about his interview with Barney Haggard, he soon began to think that he hadn't been nearly nasty enough on the subject of Drew Stilton. As soon as Drew got to hear about the discovery of the stolen goods, he began to gloat and crow about it. He'd always known that Thomas was a thief. And why hadn't the boss suspended him? What sort of role model was he for young kids? He should be arrested, thrown out of football altogether, publicly disgraced. Of course, everything that Drew said got back to Thomas which made him all the more convinced that it was Drew who was framing him.

Thomas was interviewed briefly by the police and told his story – which he had to admit sounded pretty weak and unconvincing. Everyone had been issued with a smart card for their personal locker in the new players' suite and it was a complete mystery how someone had managed to open Thomas's without his knowledge. At least it was a mystery to Thomas – the police didn't appear to think there was any mystery at all. They listened to Thomas's story with barely concealed disbelief.

Fortunately football at last came to Thomas's rescue and he was picked for the Reserve team game on Saturday – away to Barbican Pioneers. Thomas sat in the coach with Rory Betts, the reserve keeper, and Little Mac McEwan, who was also fighting his way back into the senior squad after his strange illness. And, of course, there was only one topic of conversation. Rory's theory about the Strikers burglary was that it was a just practical joke but Little Mac had another suggestion.

'There were loads of people at the reception,' said Little Mac. 'It could have been any of them. What if someone from, say, St James or Barbican wanted to upset things at Sherwood. What better way than getting a top player arrested?'

'You mean sabotage?' said Rory. 'Don't you think that's a bit way out?'

'With millions of pounds at stake if you win the Premier League, there are some people who would do anything to stop the competition, believe me.'

Thomas insisted that it was Drew and Rory was inclined to agree with him.

'There's no doubt he hates your guts,' he said. 'And he's weird enough to pull a stunt like that.'

'I've heard that Arun has been in transfer talks with Highfield Rovers over Drew. So maybe we're both right,' said Little Mac. Arun Canin was Little Mac's agent as well as Drew's.

'You mean Drew's decided to move to Rovers

and he's trying to wreck Strikers before he goes?' said Rory.

'Stranger things have happened,' said Little Mac.

All of this made concentrating on Saturday's game no easy task for Thomas. And he soon discovered that his stamina and fitness levels were causing him to struggle too. The match developed into a close fought, physical tussle with a well-organised Barbican side. But, just before half time, Thomas beat two players on the left and centred to Little Mac who volleyed the ball beautifully past the Barbican keeper. In the second half Thomas got his own name on the scoresheet after dispossessing one of the Barbican defenders just outside the box and getting in a curling shot which left the keeper stranded and went in off the angle. He was substituted soon after that and Strikers eventually ran out 2–1 winners.

As Thomas watched the players troop off the field news came through of the first team's result at Trent Park. The Reds had chalked up another win: 2–0 against Border Town. Thomas was dismayed that Drew had scored again; the other goal was a Paul Claudel penalty. The win took Sherwood into the top three of the table for the first time in nine years.

When he got to the Strikers dressing room,

Thomas found Rory speaking on his mobile. He immediately handed the phone to Thomas. 'It's Katie. Sounds as if you're in big trouble, mate.'

Thomas opened his mouth to say hello but was immediately cut down by a torrent of angry words.

'Thomas Headley, you'll be lucky if I ever speak to you again. And as for your stupid book, well you know where you can stick it. I suppose I'm the only person not to know about that crass interview, am I? Well all I can say is thank you very much for nothing and good night!'

'Wait a minute. What are you talking about?'

'I'm talking about the complete fool you've just made of yourself on the radio, talking to that mental defective, Barney Haggard. I expect Arun Canin and Drew Stilton are on the phone to their lawyers as we speak and I should imagine you'll be lucky to play for Strikers again this season after that.'

With the relief of playing football again, Thomas had totally forgotten the Barney Haggard interview.

'Oh that?'

'Yes that. You've done some stupid things since I've known you but this gets the Idiots' Oscar. How on earth did Elaine allow you to do it?'

'She didn't know.'

'I should have guessed. Well, on a personal level, how do you think I feel when you tell the world all the stories that I wouldn't even let you put in the book? And who's going to read your book now that Thomas Headley is forgotten forever in the Strikers Reserves – because if I were Joss Morecombe, I wouldn't pick you for my team if you could score ten goals every week.'

'I didn't say anything worse about Drew Stilton than he said about me.'

'So that's it. Tit for tat. I thought you were bigger than that, Thomas.'

The phone went dead and then immediately rang again.

'Yes? Is that you, Katie? I'm sorry. Believe me.'

'Is Headley there?' Thomas was shocked to recognise Joss Morecombe's voice.

'Yes . . . er . . . it's me speaking, Boss.'

'Your phone was switched off – and I can't say I blame you, Thomas. I will see you as soon as the coach arrives back at Trent Park. I'll be waiting in my office. Understood?'

'Yes.'

The journey back to Sherwood seemed the longest Thomas could ever remember. Every inch of the way he was rehearsing what he was

going to say to Joss Morecombe. Rory and Little
Mac besieged him with questions about the
Barney Haggard show and from their reactions
Thomas began to realise that he was in deep,
deep trouble.

7

NOT THE END OF THE WORLD

By the time the team coach pulled into the Trent Park stadium, Thomas's palms were sweating but cold as ice. He made his way hesitantly along the empty corridors of the Sherwood Strikers executive suite to Joss's office. The boss wasn't there, however. On the door there was a note addressed to him. He opened it and read:

I was called away. Meet me at 8 am at The Reds Coffee House by the entrance to the ground. And keep your mouth shut.

It was signed with a big squiggly 'JM'. Oh hell, said Thomas to himself. The thought of waiting twelve hours before his meeting with the manager was almost more of a torture than getting it over immediately. In a foul mood he called a taxi and went home.

The sight of Elaine didn't help matters either. 'What's the point of my trying to run your career for you when you go and do a stupid thing like this?' she said. 'I don't know what has got into you recently, Thomas. You used to be a sensible lad. But your behaviour lately has been worse than . . . than Drew Stilton even.'

The phone rang before Thomas could answer. It was a journalist ringing about the radio interview. 'This is the tenth call I've taken this evening,' hissed Elaine, holding her hand over the receiver. While she talked Thomas poured himself an orange juice and skulked off to his bedroom. His mobile rang. Oh no, thought Thomas, not another. He was about to say, Sorry, no comment, when he recognised his father's voice.

'Thomas, I heard your interview. You certainly laid it on the line, didn't you, son? And I thought you were a quiet one. Well, good on you.'

'You don't think I went over the top?'

'Is that what they're saying? Take no notice of them, son. Sometimes going over the top's the only thing to do.' Sandy's voice sounded reassuring and friendly.

'Well . . .'

'Why don't you come round to the flat to talk it over? After all, what's a father for, eh?'

'Okay,' said Thomas.

Elaine was still talking on the phone as he closed the front door behind him. He jumped into the Saab, revved the engine and, with a squeal of the tyres, scattered the pair of photographers who were gathered outside the gate under the street light. Thomas scowled and blasted the horn as he shot past. But as he turned the corner he cut his speed suddenly. A little voice of common sense told him that a traffic booking was the last thing he needed right now.

Sandy welcomed him warmly and immediately asked him about the game and his injury. Richie was out – playing football, of course. His England Junior trial was now scheduled for Wednesday night and Thomas promised he'd be there unless he was picked for the first team who had a game that evening. Eventually Sandy said, 'I hear you're seeing Joss Morecombe in the morning.'

'Yeah,' said Thomas, wondering how on earth his father knew.

'Well I think he's making a big fuss about nothing,' continued Sandy. 'You didn't say anything in that interview which struck me as irresponsible.'

'That's not what Elaine thinks.'

'It doesn't surprise me, Thomas. Elaine's

always been rather rigid in her views. That was part of the problem between us. And it's why I wonder if you're right to allow her to run your affairs. Not that I'm criticising her, mind.'

Thomas looked at his father. 'What d'you mean? I should find a new agent?'

Sandy was silent for a moment, then he slapped the arms of his chair. 'You look after your own affairs, son. I won't influence you. Young Richie's asked me to take care of his contracts and arrangements at Highfield. That's fine by me. I can handle that until he joins a senior side then he'll need a top manager, like Franco Delaney or Arun Canin.'

Thomas's mouth gaped open. How could his father seriously suggest that Richie be managed by a worm like Arun Canin. Imagine having the same agent as Cheesy Stilton! But Sandy continued, 'I know what you're thinking. And I happen to know that Mr Canin is getting fed up with Drew Stilton's antics and if the right player came along he'd be happy to drop him.'

'How do you know that? Do you know him?'

'Never met him. But I've got my contacts, Thomas. I believe Mr Canin acts for some other top players, doesn't he?'

'Yes, he's Little Mac's agent and he's got four or five other Premier League players.'

'Well, why don't you ask Little Mac – that's Lanny McEwan, isn't it? – what he thinks of Arun Canin. But as I said, don't let me influence you.'

'Elaine thinks Canin's a crook. She'd be livid if I moved to him.'

'Then maybe it's a bad idea. But you won't be living at home forever, will you, Thomas? And what happens when you move to another club – in Europe, say? I hear that Benfica are showing an interest in you. How do you like the idea of living in Rome?'

'Benfica's in Lisbon,' said Thomas.

'Yes, well. You know what I mean.'

Thomas wriggled uncomfortably. It was all too much for him to take in. He had thought of leaving Strikers – but only to get away from Drew Stilton. He didn't really want to leave the club, especially when they were on a roll. And yet all this mess he was in – the Drew Stilton business, the crazy affair of the stuff found in his locker – maybe everything could be waved away by a transfer to a big European club.

Sandy smiled reassuringly. 'Life's too short to worry about agents, son. But if you want to talk about it again, I'll be here.'

'Thanks,' said Thomas. And he meant it.

'Now if you're not strapped for cash, I wonder if you could lend me a few bob. Say fifty quid.

I'm waiting for a transfer from my bank in Scotland, you see.'

'Help yourself,' said Thomas. 'You know where my wallet is.' It wasn't the first time that he'd lent his father money in recent days, but it had only been a few quid at a time and Sandy had paid most of it back. Fifty pounds meant nothing to Thomas, anyhow. On the other hand he did feel a little uneasy at talking to Sandy about Elaine and his affairs at the club. Sandy hadn't said any more about taking the projects manager job but he seemed to know everything that was going on at Strikers. Where was he getting his information? From Monty Windsor or someone else? And then there was this sudden interest in the careers of his sons. What was his dad up to? Thomas would have liked to turn to him for advice but something held him back.

You're on your own, mate, he murmured to himself. You got yourself into all this. You get yourself out. Stop looking for people to hold your hand. Get in control, Thomas.

8
ON SONG

The interview with Joss Morecombe was less painful than he'd feared. In spite of the headlines in the tabloids and all the bad publicity for the club Joss limited himself to a short but stern lecture. He told Thomas to listen to what Elaine had to say. 'She talks a lot of sense, your mother. I can't tell you how lucky you are to have her managing you.'

Thomas didn't reply. He could see that Elaine and Joss had been talking about him and they'd decided between themselves how to deal with the situation. He felt annoyed and relieved at the same time.

'And another thing,' said Joss. 'You won't be hearing any more from the Bill about that stuff in your locker.'

'Do they know who did it?'

'No. They've exhausted their enquiries, as they

say. They agree with me that it's some sort of crack-pot practical joke and they're dropping the matter.'

'Have they talked to Drew Stilton?'

'Don't start that nonsense again, lad,' said Joss.

'But . . .'

'But nothing. Now I've some good news for you if you want to listen. You know I don't normally let team selection out of the bag. But, just this once, if you can keep it under your hat, I'll tell you.'

'What?' asked Thomas anxiously.

'That you're on the bench for Wednesday evening's fixture against Border Town.'

'That's brilliant!'

'I'm not promising you a game, mind.'

Thomas left the boss's office with a bounce in his step and the first feeling of optimism he'd had for days. And things continued to improve with a call from Katie Moncrieff.

'I'm sorry I went over the top, Thomas.'

'That's okay. I deserved it.'

'The thing is that your stupid interview has made you big news and . . . well . . . my editor wants to start serialising the Thomas Headley story as soon as possible.'

'I'm not sure.'

'He'll pay a lot of money. Is it okay if I talk to Elaine?'

'Sure. But maybe we should discuss it first? After all we haven't written it yet.'

'Good. When can I see you? How about lunch on Sunday?'

In the event Thomas didn't get a game against Border Town on Wednesday evening. He sat out the match on the bench, half disappointed that he was missing Richie's England trial, half delighted to be back in the frame for Strikers. But being on the substitutes' bench wasn't good enough – he was itching to get on to the park.

Strikers won by two goals and Drew Stilton didn't score either of them. Thomas had to agree with Rory that it was probably just as well that he and Drew weren't on the field together with so much unpleasantness flying around. Thomas kept silent in the changing room and avoided contact with Drew. He was still convinced that Cheesy had set him up over the thefts. Only a sick brain like his would think up such a thing. But he was beginning to realise that someone else must have helped him. Drew could never have done it all on his own. It was, after all, quite a clever operation to take Thomas's smart card, carry out the thefts under the noses of security and hundreds of guests and conceal everything in the locker. Perhaps Drew had hired a professional.

was su... ...that puzzled Thom... ...en his ... ...

*

Over the next few days Thomas saw a lot of his father. Richie had been the star of the England Junior trials and described every minute detail of his stunning goal over and over again. Sandy was convinced Richie would be picked for the forthcoming England Youth game against Sweden even though he was still a good few months younger that most of the other lads.

'Will you come and watch me this time?' Richie asked his brother excitedly.

'I will if I can,' said Thomas, glancing at the Strikers' fixture card. 'But if I'm back in the team I'll be in Germany.'

'I know. Bayern Munich, second leg,' said Richie glumly.

'I can't help it. It's my job,' said Thomas. 'And it'll be yours one day.'

'Sooner than anyone thinks,' said Sandy. 'I wouldn't be surprised if he were playing for Highfield in four or five seasons. And don't worry, son. I'll be at Wembley, rooting for you.'

Sandy didn't say any more about Thomas's business arrangements and he began to feel ashamed that he had questioned his father's motives. The way he was supporting Richie seemed completely genuine – just like a proper father, in fact. But there was still one thing that puzzled Thomas. When his dad had turned up in Sherwood he'd been so confident and full of himself. Now he seemed quieter and quieter by the day. Thomas sensed that something was troubling his father.

At home things were a little easier with Elaine, now that he was back to full time training. And another bonus was that he had avoided the dreaded encounter on the practice ground with Drew Stilton, because Drew was back to his old habits of flouting the club rules and not turning up for training. This time Joss wasn't having it and Drew was immediately suspended for the Saturday away game at White Hart United.

Even with Drew out of contention, Thomas still failed to get his longed-for taste of Premier League football. He wasn't brought on as a substitute by Joss because the team was playing so well – or rather, they played well right up until the final seconds. The Reds were two up in the 88th minute and coasting it, when a complete lack of concentration at the back let White Hart in to score a soft goal. In the final frantic seconds the home side threw everyone forward and forced a draw with a second scrambled goal. It was a disappointing result but it still left Strikers in the top three in the table – now just three points behind the leaders.

	P	W	L	D	F	A	Pts
West Thames Wanderers	17	10	3	4	34	13	34
Barbican	16	8	0	8	27	11	32
Sherwood Strikers	**17**	**9**	**4**	**4**	**35**	**17**	**31**
Newlynn City	17	8	4	5	30	23	29
Danebridge Forest	17	7	3	7	25	20	28
Highfield Rovers	17	8	6	3	29	22	27
Derwent Athletic	17	7	4	6	26	27	27
St James	16	7	4	5	24	21	26
White Hart United	17	6	4	7	23	18	25
Branston Town	17	6	4	7	23	22	25
Mersey United	17	7	8	2	26	29	23
Fenland Rangers	16	5	5	6	21	23	21
Kingstown Academy	17	5	7	5	24	25	20
Mersey City	17	4	6	7	19	25	19
Border Town	17	4	6	7	18	25	19
Wierdale Harriers	17	4	8	5	21	27	17
Southdown United	17	2	5	10	23	27	16
Wednesfield Royals	16	3	7	6	17	26	15
Alexandra Park	17	2	12	3	11	29	9
Wyvern Vale	17	1	12	4	10	36	7

On the Sunday Thomas had lunch with Katie Moncrieff and Paul Claudel. The Frenchman took them both to his favourite restaurant, six miles out of Sherwood, where the menu was all in French and the waiters weren't – according to Claudo.

'Just b'cause they all speak with ze funnee accent, does not mean they come from France,'

said Paul. 'I sink they all get French accent training at the English school for waiters.' He amused
himself for the rest of the meal speaking very
fast French to the waiters and revelling in their
confusion.

Katie said the Claudel book was going really
well, which was more than she could say for *The
Thomas Headley World Cup Story*.

'I sink it is best for you to write the story for
Tommee and make it all up. Who will know if it
is true or not?' said Paul.

Katie smiled. 'I know that's what most journalists are supposed to do. But I'm not like that. I
like to check the facts. And that's difficult when
the person you're supposed to be writing about
won't tell you anything.'

'It's not true,' said Thomas through a mouthful
of sausage which he suddenly realised tasted
strangely disgusting. 'I've given you a complete
tape, haven't I?'

'But it's full of things that I know already – such
as where you were staying and who scored the
goals. I want some feeling stuff. What were you
thinking when you scored that first goal? How
does an 18 year old cope with scoring twice in the
World Cup final? Are you the same person after
your World Cup experience? That sort of thing.'

'I sink you too young for this fantastic thing,

Tommee. If I score a goal in a World Cup, I write a poem to it. But you are so English.'

'I don't write poems,' said Thomas bluntly.

'Zen you should try. Listen. I write this after we beat St James.'

I was a hero here
Now it is me they fear
Swift as a deer
The defender is near
But I am jumping clear
And the ball flies from the barrel of the
    musketeer.

'Isn't the last line a bit long?' said Thomas.

'See what I mean – you English, you do not understand the poetry,' said Claudo, slapping his forehead dramatically with his hand. 'And you are not eating your treep sausage either, Tommee.'

'Treep?'

'Tripe,' translated Katie. Thomas pushed his plate away with a groan.

Later, after a glass or two of wine, he got on to the subject that was preying on his mind.

'I might be looking for a new manager some-time,' he said. 'What do you both think of Franco Delaney or Arun Canin?'

'You can't be serious. You don't want to leave

Elaine, do you?' said Katie.

'All the agents they are the bloodsuckers,' said Claudo. 'I have had maybe ten agents and they are all the same. They all want to put their hands in your pocket. Now I have one manager in France and one in England and they fight to see which one robs me the most.'

'Well they can't be worse than Arun Canin,' said Katie. 'Thomas, are you out of your mind? Elaine's doing a fantastic job for you.'

'Well, Canin doesn't do a bad job for Little Mac,' said Thomas. 'And you don't have to like your agent, do you?'

'No. I think it is better if you hate them,' said Paul Claudel with a grin.

'And I think that the best way for you to lose all your money and credibility would be to take on Arun Canin,' said Katie. 'Do you seriously want to be in the same stable as Drew Stilton?'

'I happen to know that he'd get rid of Drew if he took me on.'

'Who's been talking to you, Thomas, for heaven's sake?'

'No one. I mean, I've just been thinking Elaine doesn't have the international experience. And Sandy says . . .'

'Sandy? What's your father know about football?'

'We've just been talking. Why not? He is my dad after all.'

Katie gave him a hesitant look. 'I've been hearing strange things about him. He's got some odd chums around Sherwood, you know.'

'You mean like Monty Windsor?' said Thomas.

'Monty's all right. But some of his fellow Strikers board members are a bit dodgy. Take Donny McNail, for instance, and Frank Gardener. They both know Sandy.'

'So what? What does it matter who his friends are?'

'I don't know. Maybe you should ask yourself . . . or Sandy. You don't really know much about your father, do you, Thomas?'

On Sunday night another minor scandal shook the Strikers camp. Drew Stilton and some of his so-called mates trashed the bar at the Palm Tree. The damage was said to run to thousands of pounds and one of the waitresses was slightly injured in the ensuing fight.

Joss Morecombe acted quickly with a public statement. Drew was suspended until the police investigations were over and if he was found to be responsible for what had happened, he would be placed immediately on the transfer list. It seemed that the boss's patience with Stilton had, at last, reached its limit.

There was more good news for Thomas later in the week. He found his name was on the team sheet for the away game at Highfield Rovers. At last, he thought, I get a chance to start a game again. I've got to make this one count. It's my big chance.

The entire Headley family travelled to Highfield for the game. Richie, who wouldn't have dreamt of missing a Rovers v Strikers battle, went with his dad. Elaine travelled to the game with Katie and Jason Le Braz, who had got a slight knock in the last game and was rested.

In spite of the absence of Jason and Drew the team was a strong one.

Franco Jordan enjoyed the more attacking role and he was pushed up alongside Claudel with Pahler linking with the midfield behind him. With the wing back missing on the right Big Mac switched to the wide position. At the back, Walter Andersson had been having a highly successful introduction to the team, and he went out to the right to allow Ben El Harra to slot into the back four again.

With his first touch of the ball Thomas knew that the force was with him today. A perfect aerial pass dissecting two defenders gave Jordan a clear shot on goal, which screamed over the bar from twenty yards. From then on every run into space Thomas made attracted the passes of his team-mates like a magnet; every dummy and swerve left his markers scything at thin air; every pass was delivered with vision and perfect weight. Thomas was everywhere and playing at the very top of his game and the crowd knew it. Even the Rovers supporters seemed to be cheering him on, lifting him to new levels of skill. There was an excitement in the air, an expectation of something special.

On 30 minutes Thomas received a short through ball from Petr Pahler and nutmegged his marker as he turned. Pahler had continued his run inside Thomas and was unmarked. Thomas passed, ran diagonally across him and took the return pass without breaking his stride. There were two defenders between him and the goal; he went round the first, dummied to go round the second and cut inside. From thirty yards he unleashed a left-footed drive which at first the keeper seemed to have covered until it swerved viciously away from him into the top left corner of the goal. There were howls of joy from the Strikers fans and thunderous applause from the home crowd. Everyone on the ground knew that they had seen a really special goal that they would remember forever.

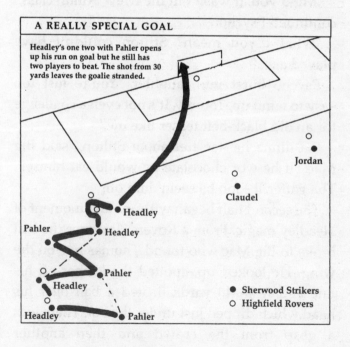

A REALLY SPECIAL GOAL

Headley's one two with Pahler opens up his run on goal but he still has two players to beat. The shot from 30 yards leaves the goalie stranded.

Jordan

Claudel

Headley

Pahler

Headley

Pahler

Headley

Headley

Pahler

● Sherwood Strikers
○ Highfield Rovers

But Highfield Rovers were not a side to give up when they were one–nil down and they attacked the Strikers goal furiously in the run-up to half time. Only a stunning dive by Sean Pincher, followed by an even better save with his legs from a close range Graham Deek volley, kept his team ahead at the interval.

'You're on fire today, DD,' said Psycho to Thomas at half time. 'What did you have for breakfast? A curry?'

Thomas smiled.

'Mind you, it wasn't in the Drew Stilton class,' continued Psycho.

'What d'you mean? Stilton couldn't have played a . . .'

Psycho burst into laughter. 'You're just too easy to wind up, Tommy. It's not even a challenge for an old black-belt teaser like me.'

'Ya dinna ha' tae fret aboot Stilton,' said Big Mac. 'If he wor chocolate he would eat himsel'. Tha gaffer'll soon be seein' him off.'

The second half began with another moment of Headley magic. From a Rovers clearance the ball broke to Big Mac who found Thomas free on the wing. He looked up, spotted the keeper off his line and from 40 yards floated a ball over his head which dipped just under the bar. There was a gasp from the crowd and then another monstrous roar as the fans cherished another moment of pure skill.

Nil–two. And the Thomas Headley show continued. He headed just wide as he ran in to meet a low cross. Then a free kick from well outside the area curled round the wall, beat the goalie and hit the post.

At the other end Deekie went close with a volley after he'd been put through by Mattie Barry and then Franco Jordan missed for Strikers on the break when he had an open goal to shoot at. With minutes to go, Thomas won the ball in the tackle and darted between two defenders. He lifted it over the centre back as he advanced on him, and into the path of Paul Claudel whose first-time shot on goal was too fierce for the keeper to hold. He parried it and Thomas was the first to react to the loose ball. He was on it like a terrier. The keeper threw himself to his right to block the shot and Thomas jinked to the left and sidestepped the ball into the net.

The entire ground rose to greet the hat trick from Headley the master. Little Richie, high in the stand behind the goal, clapped until his hands were sore. 'I don't mind losing if we lose to the best player in England,' he said to his father. 'And the best thing about it is, he's *my brother*!'

*

After the game Thomas joined Elaine, Katie and Jason for the journey home. On his way to the supporters' bar, where they'd agreed to meet, he was surrounded by young Strikers supporters desperate for his autograph. They wanted to talk about the game and Thomas didn't have the heart to walk away from his young fans. As he was signing books, shirts, scraps of paper, anything that came to hand, he suddenly noticed his father standing in the shadows talking intently to a group of men. He was about to walk over to greet him when he noticed that one of the people in the group was Arun Canin. He thought he recognised a couple of the others, too, but he wasn't sure. Katie's words came to his mind. 'You don't really know much about your father, do you?' Thomas turned away and went into the supporters' bar.

9
HITTING THE WALL

'One hundred and forty-eight, one hundred and forty-nine, one hundred and fifty. See, you can still do it, DD!'

Jason Le Braz stood over his friend clicking off the scores into his iPhone. Thomas raised himself wearily from the gym floor. Getting back to peak fitness was no fun at all, until you achieved it. The road there was a long hard slog and Thomas hated press-ups more than anything. He made a mental note to ask Doc Martin if he could replace them with a different exercise on his fitness programme. Now for the weights. As he and Jason did trunk curls with 15 kilo dumbbells on their shoulders, Thomas tried hard to think of something to look forward to.

'Why don't we go along to that new place in the Horsefair tonight?' he grunted.

'You mean Hank's Tank? It sounds okay.'

Hank's Tank was Sherwood's latest club, a shiny metal underground room like the inside of a vast submarine, with several different decks. It had three live bands every night and was bringing in big crowds since its opening three weeks ago. Hank's belonged to one of Strikers' board directors, Donald McNail. Thomas had never met Donny, as he was called, but he knew that, as well as his interest in Strikers, he was a wealthy property developer and a very shrewd and successful businessman. And he knew the pulling power of football stars, which was why he had issued the entire team with free membership to Hank's Tank.

'I've got to put in some work on that stupid book first,' said Thomas. 'Katie's been nagging me about it again. It's supposed to come out soon after Christmas and we haven't got to the quarter-finals yet. And you know how I hate being tied down like this.'

'Well, if it's tying down you need, she's just arrived with the right gear.'

Thomas turned and saw Katie standing at the door of the gym. She had a coil of multi-coloured rope slung over her shoulder.

'Oh, hell,' said Thomas. 'I mean, uh, great . . . I said I'd go climbing with her this afternoon. Just what I need after all those press-ups.'

*

An hour later, Thomas Headley was ten metres up a slab of smooth wall which had little rock-shaped hand holds like lumps of cold rice pudding jutting out of it. He was clinging on by his fingers and toes and feeling the sweat trickling gently down his spine. Somewhere above him Katie was shouting instructions and climbing as effortlessly as if she was on a stepladder. Thomas noticed for the first time that she had a tattoo of what looked like a thistle on her left shoulder.

Below the instructor was taking up the slack on the belay rope which was attached to Thomas's harness via the anchor point at the top of the wall above him. As Thomas climbed the instructor pulled on the rope, so that if he fell he would be held by the harness. That was the theory; in practice the terror of falling wiped everything from Thomas's mind as he concentrated on the next hold and hauled himself into another uncomfortable position against the wall. As he gasped for breath he mentally ticked off another hobby he wouldn't be taking up; he'd very suddenly decided that he didn't like heights and he certainly didn't enjoy the feeling of having his fingers and arms pulled out of their sockets. His hands were getting sweatier. He looked down and gasped at the distance from the floor and his whole body started to shake. As he reached out for another hold, his grip went and with a loud cry he fell backwards. The safety rope went taut and he swung in a small arc against the wall, grazing his shoulder. He'd had enough. Thomas called out to the instructor and was gently lowered to the ground on the belay rope. Katie scrambled down the wall to join him.

'Not bad for a beginner,' she laughed.

'Well I'm staying a beginner; I'm not doing that again.'

'Why not?'

Thomas wasn't going to own up to Katie that he was scared of heights, so he made a joke of it. 'I've got too many things to do right now – such as writing a book with this bossy journalist,' he said.

'That's a pity. I was hoping you'd come to the Peak District with me next week. There's a special beginners' course. And there'll be some bungee jumping, too.' Thomas felt his stomach heave. He had already decided that if he ever found a hobby to take his mind off football, it was going to be strictly at ground level.

Afterwards, in the café of the Craggy Park climbing school, Thomas gulped down a much

needed pint of fresh orange juice and told Katie
his latest news – beginning with the encounter
with his father and Arun Canin after the Rovers
game.

'I phoned Sandy last night,' said Thomas.

'And what did he say?'

'That's the strange thing. First of all he denied
he'd been with Arun Canin at all. Then he said
that he'd just bumped into a bunch of mates
while Richie was talking to Graham Deek and
some of the other Rovers players, and it was
possible that Arun Canin might have been with
them.'

'And you think he was lying?'

'I guess so. And then he said something very
odd.'

'What?'

'He said, "I want you to tell Richie that I'd do
anything for him. He's the greatest and I'm glad
I've been a father to him – if only for a week or
two." And then he hung up.'

'And you haven't heard from him since?'

'No. Maybe I'll go round tonight.'

'Weird. What's Canin up to, I wonder? There's
nothing that man wouldn't do to make a few
quid.'

'Yeah, I was never really serious about him
being my agent.'

'You're staying with Elaine?'

'Yes. She's had this great idea. She's going to hire someone to work with her who knows all about international sponsorships and can do the road work. Joss Morecombe says he knows just the right guy.'

'Thank heavens for that. You'd have been crazy to leave Elaine. By the way, what's happening about Drew Stilton? Is there any more news?'

'He's still on the transfer list, but no one's seen him since last week. I bet he's on the booze again. Or else he thinks the police are after him for that stupid trick he played on me.'

'You mean the locker room mystery? I don't think Drew did that. It's not his style. Drew's idea of a practical joke is to let all your tyres down and put sugar in your petrol tank and then torch the car.'

'Then who was it?'

'I'm not sure. Let's just say I've got my suspicions.'

Thomas nearly changed his mind about going along to the Tank that evening; training and the rock climbing had left him completely wiped out. Then he thought that maybe he'd call in at Sandy's flat on the way to have a chat with him and Richie. The flat was locked and there was no sign of life, so Thomas left a note saying he would call later and went on to his rendezvous with Rory and Jason.

As he entered Hank's Tank half the heads in the room turned towards him. There was a lot of whispering and pointing as usual, but he was well used to his celebrity status by now and he took no notice. A girl who seemed a bit drunk ran up to him and asked for his autograph. He scribbled his signature on a piece of paper while she giggled and waved to her friends. He saw Rory and Jason at a table with a crowd of people and he was about to join them when someone tapped him on the shoulder.

'Eh, excuse me, sir. It's Mr Headley, isn't it?' said a stocky, bald man in a dinner jacket.

'Yes.'

'I'm the manager of Hank's. I wonder, before you join your friends, if you could spare a moment to meet Mr McNail, our owner? He'd very much like to welcome you to the establishment.'

What's going on? wondered Thomas as he was led through a silver-panelled door into a very flash office. Behind an enormous desk sat Donny McNail. Thomas immediately recognised the tall man with longish greying hair and enormous eyebrows as one of the people whom he had seen talking to his father and Arun Canin at Highfield Rovers the other night.

'Thomas, we meet at last. Good of you to come. A drink?'

Thomas politely refused.

'You'll be wondering why I invited you, Thomas. So I'll come straight to the point. You see, I want to know if you've seen your father recently?'

'Sandy?'

'Yes, Sandy.'

'You're a friend of his, aren't you, Mr McNail?'

'Call me Donny – everyone does. You could say that Sandy and I are friends – perhaps business associates would be more accurate. Have you seen him?'

'Not since . . . not for a few days,' said Thomas, wondering what all this was about.

'Well, you may know he's been staying in an apartment of mine in town. And now he seems to have, well, departed. And he owes me rather a lot of money.'

'How much?'

'A little over fifty thousand pounds. And I mean to get it back.'

Thomas whistled softly but for some reason he wasn't totally surprised. His first thoughts were for Richie. Was he safe? Had he gone with his father? Where were they? He brought the conversation with Donny McNail to a rapid close, promising that he would try and track down his father, and left the club without a word to Jason and Rory. Outside he called Elaine on his mobile.

'You seen Richie?'

'Yes, he's here. He arrived an hour ago with all his things. He says your father's had to go back to Scotland. He's left a letter for you. Where are you now?'

'I'm on my way home. See you in half an hour.'

10
SUPER SUB

My dear Tommy,

By the time you read this I'll be out of your life for good. Elaine was right to be suspicious about me and my reasons for coming to Sherwood. You see, I was so hopelessly in debt and I needed some money very badly. Your dad's a bit of a con-man, I'm afraid – I'm glad you take after your mum.

I was a fool, too. I might have known that nothing Arun Canin does is quite what it seems. I've known him for many years and he's always been bent – crooked through and through. He told me his big plan was to dump Drew Stilton and make a fortune from managing you. If I could get you to agree, I would get a share of the action. My job was to persuade you and to undermine Elaine in your eyes. And, yes, I 'borrowed' that card from your wallet for him, and then replaced it. I didn't even know it was a key and I certainly didn't suspect he was going to pull a stunt like that and set you up as a thief.

He was doing everything he could to make you walk out on Strikers, you see. When I found out he was using me to frame my own son, I wanted to tell you everything. But that meant telling Richie, too, and I didn't want him to leave me — we've got on so well these last few weeks.

But today I realised I couldn't live with it. Tell Richie about it in your own way. But tell him I love him. I love both of you.

Yours for ever
Sandy

Thomas passed the letter to his mother without a word. She read it, frowning. 'Hmm. I can't say I'm surprised,' she snorted. 'Trouble is that your father's so plausible he can even convince himself.'

'I honestly believe it will break his heart to leave Richie.'

'Maybe. But you're well shot of him, I tell you.'

'What shall I say to Richie?'

'It's up to you.'

'Then I'm going to burn this and tell him that Sandy's gone away on business.'

'Do you think he'll believe you?'

'Probably not but he doesn't need this right

now. It's best he remembers the good side of his dad. Where is he?'

'Upstairs in bed. He was exhausted when he came in. He heard today that he would be playing in the Youth International against Sweden. And then when he rushed back to tell Sandy, he'd gone, of course.'

'When is the game?'

'The same day as your return leg against Bayern Munich. If you don't mind I'll go and watch Richie instead of coming to Germany with you.'

'Of course. What are we going to do about Canin?'

'*You*'re going to do nothing. You'll leave it to your agent. Understood?' Elaine smiled for the first time and put her arm round Thomas's shoulder.

*

Bayem had given Strikers a big shock in the home leg of the UEFA Cup, sneaking two breakaway goals in the second half, completely against the run of play. Since then, Strikers' luck had been rather up and down. The worst thing to happen was a serious ankle injury to Brad Trainor. It happened in the table game at Kingstown Academy where Strikers snatched victory in the final minute to run out 2–1 winners. Kingstown were a hard, physical side and a couple of other players, Thomas included, sustained slight knocks in the game too. As a result Joss rested Thomas, Pasta and Big Mac for the weekend derby battle with Danebridge. The reserve players rose to the occasion and a Strikers side with one eye on the European game on the following Wednesday nevertheless handed out a real thrashing to their neighbours. The 4–0 scoreline didn't flatter them. Paul Claudel scored twice before he was substituted and then Little Mac proved that he was back to full fitness and form with two more goals in the second half. The victory took Strikers to the top of the league for the first time in a decade.

But there remained one big question that the entire football world was asking. Although Strikers were close to becoming one of the best clubs in England again, were they good enough to hold their own in Europe? They had played well enough against Bayern – but the result of the first leg seemed to suggest that the answer was still no. A great deal of pride was at stake in the return game and, though it seemed unlikely that they could reverse the 2–0 deficit against the leaders of the *Bundesliga*, the Reds still needed to put on a truly great and gutsy performance. To lose would be a big blow to the team spirit that Joss Morecombe had created' at Sherwood. To

	P	W	L	D	F	A	Pts
Sherwood Strikers	20	12	4	4	44	19	40
West Thames Wanderers	20	11	3	6	39	15	39
Barbican	19	10	0	9	30	12	39
St James	19	10	4	5	29	22	35
Highfield Rovers	20	10	7	3	33	26	33
Newlynn City	20	9	5	6	32	25	33
Derwent Athletic	20	8	4	8	30	28	32
Danebridge Forest	20	8	5	7	26	26	31
Mersey United	20	8	8	4	33	32	28
White Hart United	20	6	5	9	25	24	27
Branston Town	19	6	5	8	24	25	26
Mersey City	20	5	7	8	24	29	23
Fenland Rangers	19	5	7	7	26	25	22
Wierdale Harriers	20	5	8	7	25	29	22
Kingstown Academy	19	5	9	5	26	31	20
Border Town	20	4	8	8	19	31	20
Wednesfield Royals	19	3	8	8	20	30	17
Southdown United	20	2	8	10	23	33	16
Alexandra Park	20	3	13	4	12	34	13
Wyvern Vale	20	2	14	4	11	45	10

draw would be just about acceptable. But every member of the team believed they could win.

The important thing was to prevent the Germans from scoring again in the opening quarter of the game. So Joss opted for a fairly defensive plan with plenty of attacking alternatives waiting on the bench, ready to come on in the second half.

Sean Pincher

Jason Le Braz   Walter Andersson   Dean Oldie   Ben El Harra

Jamie MacLachlan   Cosimo Lagattello   Thomas Headley

Sergio Gambolini   Petr Pahler

Paul Claudel

Reserves: Rory Betts, Tarquin Kelly, Francisco Panto-Gomes, Franco Jordan, Lanny McEwan.

Thomas liked Munich. The city was relaxed and full of interest with its astonishing medieval buildings, most of them Bierkellers and bars - the Germans seemed to like their beer even more than the English. 'Good job Cheesy's not here,' joked Psycho. 'We'd never get him out of the boozers.' The hotel Schwarzkopf was brilliant. Even the weather was good for midwinter. And the practice ground was one of the best any of the players had seen.

Thomas had been pleased with the way that Richie had coped with Sandy's departure.

Maybe the England v Sweden Youth game had taken his mind off it. Thomas was a little sad that he wasn't travelling down to Wembley with Richie and Elaine for the big game but Elaine had promised to ring him with the result as soon as it was over.

Media interest in the Bayern v Strikers game was phenomenal. It seemed that the army of the team's followers from the press, radio and television grew with every game Strikers played in Europe. Most of them were in a big hotel on the other side of the city, but the photographers seemed to be permanently staked out around the Schwarzkopf or the practice centre, where the very well-organised stewards and security guards kept them at a distance except for official photocalls.

Katie complained about the security when she finally managed to meet the boys for a drink in a bar on the evening before the game. 'I've tried everything I know,' she told Thomas, Jason and Rory. 'I've done disguises, bribes, charm even but these Germans are amazing. And they are so polite when they kick you out, too. That almost makes it worse.'

'It's nice and peaceful in the hotel for once, with the hacks kept in check,' said Jason with a chuckle.

'What about the game? Are you going to win?' asked Katie.

'What do you think?' said Rory.

'I've got £10 on a 3–0 win for Strikers,' said Katie. 'If I win I get nearly £300.'

'We'll do our best for you,' said Jason. 'But what if it's 3–0 and I'm standing with the ball in front of an empty goal? Do I blast it over the bar just so that you can win your bet?'

'Of course not, stupid,' she smiled. 'If you win 10–0 I'll be even happier.'

Katie managed to have a quiet word with Thomas before the team-mates returned to the hotel. She told him that the word was out that Little Mac had sacked Arun Canin as his manager. 'That just leaves him with Drew Stilton at Strikers, and he's welcome to Drew,' she said. 'The way things are no one's interested in buying him right now. So he might stay on the transfer list for the rest of his life or until his contract runs out. Imagine being on the scrap heap aged 18!'

Thomas had told Katie the full story about Sandy. She was a little surprised to learn of his involvement in the thefts but she said that she had suspected Arun Canin all along. 'It's a pity there's not enough evidence for the police to pick him up,' she said.

*

Thomas tried hard to put all the business of Sandy and Arun Canin out of his head for the big game. As he ran out on to the turf of the imposing Allianz Arena the roar went up from the noisy and expectant crowd. There were at least 10,000 Strikers fans in the ground and plenty more outside, and they were making almost as much din as the Munich supporters. Fears of trouble in the *Bierkellers* of Munich had come to virtually nothing, with only a handful of arrests. The Reds supporters had come to enjoy themselves; they knew they were the underdogs, but they were intending to have a night to remember and they were singing at the tops of their voices.

> 'Blue Moon
> You've started singing too soon
> Although you beat us two-none
> You'll be so sick when we've won.'

Bayern were in their away-strip, even though they were playing at home, and it didn't do them any favours – grey shirts with green and white hoops and purple shorts. It was so awful that you had to wonder whether it had been designed to put the opposition off.

The pitch shone emerald green in the powerful lights. It was quite grassy and rather heavy and both teams took a little time to settle and find the length of their passes. The scrappy early play wasn't helped by the referee who seemed determined to stamp his authority on the game by handing out yellow cards like confetti. First the big Bayern central defender, Braun, went in the book for a late tackle on Claudel. Then, in quick succession, Dean Oldie, Jason Le Braz and Bayern's Russian striker, Ventinoff, were carded – all for minor fouls which hardly deserved a booking. That psyched the crowd up even more and the Reds' fans roared out another song:

'We love to go a-wandering
Along the cliffs of Dover
And if we see you, referee,
We'll kick you over, and over, and over.'

Bayern were awarded a free kick just outside the Reds' penalty area and Ventinoff's fierce, curling shot was brilliantly punched clear by Sean Pincher. Jason picked it up on the right and jinked down the wing before finding Thomas with a wonderful long ball across the entire width of the park. Thomas then dummied to go inside and beat his man down the wing. His cross took a deflection off Braun who had tried to close him down and let Petr Pahler in' for a shot on goal which the keeper just reached and touched round the post for a corner. Big Mac took it and Paul Claudel rose at the near post and flicked on to Gambolini who buried the ball in the back of the German net. The keeper had no chance.

Suddenly the players and the crowd realised that Strikers were back in the tie. The tempo of the game quickened and the noise grew to an ear-splitting roar, punctuated by the German klaxons and whistles. With the Reds' midfield now dominating, the Bayem Munich goal was under some pressure but the keeper, Hesse, completed a brilliant first half performance with an astonishing reaction save from a close-range Claudel volley and the teams went in at half time with the score still 1-0 in Strikers' favour.

'I'm running around like a rabbit,' gasped Psycho, slumping back in a chair in the dressing room.

'More like a rottweiler than a rabbit,' said Sean Pincher. 'You take care, Deano. We don't want to play the second half with ten men.'

Joss Morecombe walked in with Len Dallal. 'I'm bringing on Jordan up front,' he said brusquely. 'That means you're off, Sergio. Sorry but we need two more goals.'

The Italian nodded. Like the other players, Sergio Gambolini had learnt to accept the boss's decisions without complaint.

'One more careless tackle and you're off too, Dean,' added Joss.

'Okay, Boss,' said Psycho.

A phone rang and Thomas realised it was his. The boss glared at him – all the players were under strict instructions to turn off their mobiles during games. But Thomas quickly picked up his phone and listened.

'Brilliant!' He turned to the other players. 'England beat Sweden 2–0. And Richie scored the first goal.' A cheer rippled round the dressing room and Joss allowed himself a little smile.

'Now perhaps we can get back to the little job we're supposed to be doing,' he said sarcastically. 'We're playing 4–3–3 from now on and I want Petr to push up with Franco and Paul. And maybe you'll try and play as well as your brother, Headley.'

Strikers continued to attack in the second half but the German defence was even better organised than before and they were very dangerous on the break. On the hour Ventinoff broke clear of Dean Oldic and fired a thunderbolt which Sean somehow got a hand to and touched over the bar. The seconds ticked away. Twenty minutes to go, then ten. There seemed no way through the tight Bayern defence and one or two of the players were giving up on the patient build-ups and resorting in desperation to hopeful long balls aimed at the head of Franco Jordan. The threat of the break grew stronger as Jason Le Braz and Thomas committed themselves to attack and Psycho tired at the back. Eventually Joss had to take him off and with five minutes to go he went for a double substitution. Tarquin Kelly replaced Psycho and Little Mac McEwan came on instead of Petr Pahler. The switch up front, with Little Mac on the right, Claudo on the left and Franco down the centre, gave the attack fresh urgency. Suddenly there was just a touch of panic in the German back four. Little Mac hit the post with a snap shot from the edge of the area and a Franco header went just wide.

Thomas picked up the Bayern keeper's goal kick in his own half and found Big Mac running through the centre. He belted down the left wing for the return pass but instead saw Big Mac lift the ball over the head of the German centre back to Claudel, who shaped to turn his defender and instead back-heeled the ball into the path of Little Mac, coming in behind him. The sub's shot was straight and true and, for once, Hesse couldn't get near it.

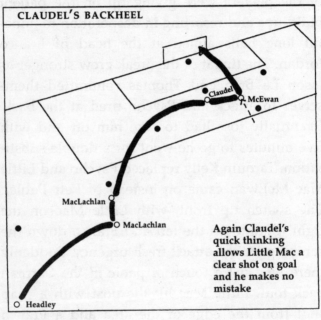

CLAUDEL'S BACKHEEL

Claudel

McEwan

MacLachlan

MacLachlan

Again Claudel's quick thinking allows Little Mac a clear shot on goal and he makes no mistake

Headley

● Bayern Munich
○ Sherwood Strikers

Thomas stood and punched the air as the ball drilled into the back of the net. Then he raced in and joined the others who were mobbing Little Mac.

There was just time to re-start before the ref's whistle blew for the end of 90 minutes.

11
EXTRA TIME

Thomas hardly heard a word of the team talk Joss Morecombe gave out on the pitch before extra time began. The crowd was making so much noise that it was difficult to hear a thing and, anyway, he wasn't really listening. He couldn't remember when he'd last felt so psyched up in a game – probably in the World Cup final. The players were knackered but they knew that one goal would do it and they all wore the same look of determination.

On the re-start Strikers again attacked the goal in front of their supporters and the fans roared them on – it was amazing that any of them still had a voice left but they shouted and screamed and sang as first Big Mac fired over the bar and then Franco Jordan's shot was well saved by Hesse. Then Pasta Lagattello was dispossessed just inside the Bayern half and a sharp pass put Ventinoff in the clear. It was one-on-one with Sean Pincher and the Russian forward kept his nerve and put the ball under the keeper's body and into the back of the net.

Now it was the turn of the Munich fans to cheer and hoot their klaxons and in what seemed like seconds, the first 15 minutes of extra time were over and Strikers, after all their good work, were staring defeat in the face. Thomas knew the Germans would get all their men behind the ball for the last quarter of an hour and he resolved to run at the defenders whenever he could. His first charge on goal ended with a clattering tackle just outside the angle of the area and Claudo stepped up to take the set-piece with Thomas alongside him. Thomas ran in and dummied a left-footed shot over the wall and Claudo immediately hit it with his right. The ball curled low around the wall and bounced wickedly in front of Hesse who picked up the flight at the last moment and managed to flap at it with both hands. Thomas had continued his run past the wall and the ball dropped on to his weaker right foot. On the half-volley he cracked it at the German goal and it flew past a despairing Hesse into the net. From the other end the Reds' supporters' roar again filled the night sky and Thomas picked the ball out of the back of the net and kicked it triumphantly in their direction.

Three–three. The three away goals put Strikers ahead but there was no way that they could suddenly switch from out-and-out attack to solid defence. Now it was end to end stuff. Patient build-ups were forgotten as the Red tide flowed forward in attack and then poured back to defend desperately as Bayern Munich took their turn to assault the Strikers' goal. Sean touched over when the entire home crowd had already gone up for a goal and an immense groan echoed round the stadium. Sean caught the ball from the corner and his kick reached Big Mac on the halfway line. He looked up and saw Jason haring down the right touchline and found him with a measured pass. In turn Jason hit a first-time diagonal ball into the box. The big central defender went up with Paul Claudel and headed it away for a corner.

Thomas approached the corner flag to take it and Big Mac came over to him.

'Ah'm goany poot big Tarkie on the near post an Ah'll come in wi wee Jason way oot on the far, d'yer ken.' He ran off leaving Thomas to puzzle out what he meant. Seeing Tarquin Kelly pushing his weight about on the near post, Thomas realised he was the decoy. Big Mac and Jason Le Braz were both lurking wide on the right and, as Thomas curled his weighted left-footed corner over the goal mouth and over the keeper, they both ran in on it. Jason got to it with his head and made good, sharp contact. It was on target but the keeper managed to turn, twist to his right, dive and deflect the ball out and away along the goal line. Thomas, racing in from the left, was the first to it. With a touch of his left foot he flicked it up, sidestepped the sliding tackle of a German defender and hit the ball with his right before it landed. It felt good, really good. And it was. The keeper, still on his knees, watched the shot fly over his head into the top right-hand corner. Thomas lay spread-eagled on the ground and one by one his team-mates leapt on top of him. They had won. There was no way that Bayern were coming back from that with two minutes to go. And the Strikers fans let them know it.

> 'Our eyes have seen our DD score
> A third and then a fourth
> And the Reds go marching on!'

As the final whistle sounded Joss Morecombe came out of the dug-out with his hands raised to the heavens. He had just witnessed the bravest and the most inspirational performance he'd ever seen from a team under his control. Strikers had won 4-1 away from home against one of the best in Europe. And he knew, and the supporters at the far end knew, that this team had just announced its return amongst the elite of the world stage. The Reds were back!

Results:

Sherwood Strikers 2 West Thames Wanderers 0
Real Madrid 2 – Sherwood Strikers 2
   (UEFA Cup)
St James 1 – Sherwood Strikers 3
Sherwood Strikers 4 – Mersey United 1
Sherwood Strikers 7 – Dawlston Albion 1
   (FA Cup)
Sherwood Strikers 2 – Border Town 0
White Hart United 2 – Sherwood Strikers 2
Highfield Rovers 1 – Sherwood Strikers 3
   (Headley 3)
Sherwood Strikers 0 – Bayern Munich 2
   (UEFA Cup)
Kingstown Academy 1 – Sherwood Strikers 2
Sherwood Strikers 4 – Danebridge Forest 0
Bayern Munich 1 – Sherwood Strikers 4 a.e.t
   (UEFA Cup)